# RAILROAD
# REDEMPTION

by

## WYNETTE I. MELLEN

&

## A. WYNETTE ROBERTSON

StoneHouse Ink  2010

StoneHouse Ink
Nampa ID 83686
www.TheStonePublishingHouse.com

First Hardcover Edition: February 2010
First Paperback Edition: February 2010

Mellen I. Wynette,
Railroad Redemption: a novel/by Wynette I. Mellen. -1st. ed.

Library of Congress Control Number:  2010922875

ISBN 978-0982607831 (Paperback)

Cover design by Andrew Garcia

Printed in the United States of America

## STONEHOUSE INK

*To all those who have a dream.*
*To Dr. A.E. Cudmore and Virginia Armstrong*
*who encouraged the original author.*

# RAILROAD
# REDEMPTION

# INTRODUCTION

ALL THE MILES THE wheels turned on the asphalt testified of a journey filled with joy and anticipation. Granna would sit between my brother and me in the back seat and all my childhood years I looked forward to the trip. It was filled with stories of Dad's family and a little of Mom's family. Dad's family was way more interesting: Railroaders, ranchers, sinners, saints. Mom's family was boring...or at least what we knew of their tales. Piling into our silver LTD Ford with its blue interior at our home in Nampa, the expected stories began before the rest stop outside of Boise and ended when we pulled into the Glenns Ferry cemetery, or they began on the journey back at about Mountain Home. All the exceptionally good stories lasted the entire trip until it finally brought us back to our beds where Granna tucked us in.

The Federal-Aid Highway Act of 1956 was to produce easier transportation across this beloved land. The towns that dotted along the old highway were reduced to a mere exit sign. Still today, thousands of vehicles pass by King Hill and Glenns Ferry with little or no recognition of their existence. But for me, even now that I have grown, they represent all that is good and wholesome in America. When Granna raised her family, life seemed to me to be a simple time, a moral time, a time of faith and virtue, a time where these two towns bustled with activity. I could have very well grown up here had the Union Pacific Railroad not split the Round House to Nampa and Pocatello.

The family legacy still haunts my soul like the aroma of a newly budded iris. Here the Snake River winds its peaceful yet treacherous path, cutting through the welcoming valley that lays below flat mountain tops, lush and green in the spring, dry and golden brown in the fall, holding faithfully the treasures of a by-gone era.

Memorial Day weekend was the best time for the family stories. As is tradition, either my brother or I would ask Dad or Granna about a person we had just honored with flowers. Of course, neither would ever need a request because both were always too eager to tell us tales of King Hill and Glenn's Ferry. One gravestone in particular always seemed to aggravate Dad.

Forrest, "Forrey", O'Brien had died in the Korean War, and every year Dad would bring an American Flag to put on his grave. The Veteran Services had been contacted countless times, and although Dad was assured they would get a flag on Forrey's grave, each year his grave lay bare and forgotten.

The family was transformed the summer Forrey died. So often the death of a loved one leaves an individual and even an entire family with an empty void, but every once in a while, that void is soothed and filled with unexpected gifts. Forrey didn't live his life in any miraculous way he just loved his family.

# CHAPTER 1

I HAVE HEARD THAT men who come home from war are never comfortable with expressing emotions of sorrow. Until Forrey's death, his sister, Avelle, was never comfortable expressing her emotions of sorrow either. So in 1951 it was a surprise when her friend and neighbor, Maud Warnick, saw Avelle sitting on the broad front stoop that faced the highway.

Avelle sat with her forearms resting on her knees, hands folded, drained with a wilted emptiness. The late afternoon sun begged Avelle to lift her head. Looking on either side of the stoop, she noticed the tight spiral of buds on the morning glory vines climbing up the porch rails. Half hidden in the fallen leaves was a little ragged shoe and a worn and discarded rag doll. Really! She *must* pull herself together soon and rake the yard.

Not twenty feet away, a car went by on the highway, and a little blond boy waved to her from the back seat. With a tender smile, Avelle waved back, and watched the car disappear from her sight and her world. A scalding tear found its way from her eye and traced slowly down her cheek. She put out her tongue to catch it and was surprised at its saltiness. All of a sudden she was conscious of her appearance, her disheveled hair, her swollen and tear-stained face. She could never cry prettily, but most always splotch and blotch, hiccup and gasp. Afterward this empty feeling was accompanied by a lousy headache. Today the headache matched the ache in her heart. There was aspirin in the house and she sort of remembered taking a couple when she woke crying at dawn. "Why wasn't there an aspirin to take the pain from her heart?" She knew; however, that when the sting of grief bites you like a rabid dog, expressions of sorrow must be given their proper place or the grief will never heal.

From inside the quiet home the clock struck four o'clock with foreboding chimes and confirmed to Avelle that the world she had known was now at an end. Another tear started. She jumped up and ran into the house as if rising to the call to defend her family from any more deadly invaders.

As the screen door slammed behind her, Avelle realized Maud's kitchen curtain had twitched when she ran in and a barb of annoyance pricked her mind. She didn't need watched over, for Heaven's sake!

Inside the Warnick's home Maud turned from her window and paced her kitchen floor and said, "Poor kid.

She's gone inside now, should I go over do you think, and ask her to dinner? Or, no, maybe I better wait and ask Charlie first, though she did seem to have a little spunk just now. I don't think she was crying again. Probably she smelled something burning or something else, maybe. But I'll go over if you think I should, Frank?" Frank just grunted, not looking up from the Sunday paper, knowing that she didn't expect nor want an answer.

Avelle stood on the worn checkered linoleum feeling the silence of the child-remembered house wrapping about her like a comfortable old shawl. The words of her mother's favorite old poem, "A little house where love has dwelt, and friendship is a guest..." brought comfort without actually rising to the surface.

She glanced at the bathtub Charlie had insisted on for their family's comfort. Was there any warm water? The old monster of a coal stove had a reservoir on the back that held ten gallons and kept plenty of warm water on hand *if* she remembered to fill it. She had a special bucket that wasn't supposed to be used for anything but filling the reservoir. Let's see...had she set it back in the tub? Yes! There it was. Avelle took the small saucepan she used for a dipper, and to her relief found on lifting the lid, that the reservoir was full of good, warm, water.

It was just a step from the stove to the tub, for Charlie had put the tub into what had been the pantry. For perhaps the thousandth time she wondered what her mother would have thought of this unorthodox act of Charlie's. She barely remembered her mother, yet she convinced herself that the little she could remember had a tremendous influence on her life.

The Section House they lived in was set aside by the Railroad Company for the use of their foreman. The Foreman, Fred Davis, was a bachelor who decided to board on the other side of the highway and insisted Charlie move his family in. It was strictly forbidden, without written permission, to make any change to the home no matter how slight or particular. So Charlie, who by rights shouldn't have been living in the house in the first place, had taken it upon himself to set a tub into the pantry she never used anyway.

Charlie had been raised on a ranch, and didn't have any idea of the sanctity of Company property. It is drilled into Company children even before they learn to walk. Scandalized by the very thought, she had tried to talk her young husband out of his intent to provide them the convenience of a tub. He was for once adamant, and finally the comfort out-weighed the fear of the Inspector, and she was only too glad. Like now she was rubbing a soapy cloth over her swollen face, relaxing in the warm water, refreshing and reviving her. Although time seemed to stand still, the only indication of how much time truly passed was the confession of the water getting scummy and becoming barely lukewarm.

Even though Avelle lay there finally allowing herself some comfort, her mind plagued her with unneeded worry. She knew, of course, Charlie would keep a keen eye on their children as they played at her folk's home. Yet Avelle also knew Aunt Nell never saw a thing, even right under her nose.

Teddy and the littlest twins played in the street more than in the yard, and never once had she heard them being called back.

Suddenly feeling isolated, Avelle's foot slipped in the water as she jumped up causing her to almost fall back into the tub. Vigorously toweling off the soapy water, then balancing precariously on one foot, she slid into the fresh underclothing as she stepped from the tub. Uck! What a mess! Was all of that on her? No wonder she felt better now. Cautiously peeking around as if sneaking through the empty house without being seen, she dashed into the bedroom. Avelle questioned the construction of the house the Company expected their men to live in, (especially those with families). The framed construction was built without closets, kitchen cupboards, and the smelly old outside privies. Oh well, Avelle thought, they were lucky not to be paying rent somewhere for a while.

Without an extensive wardrobe, she easily decided on her nice new navy linen dress. After all, it was Sunday. With slipper straps flapping, she came back into the kitchen to the only decent mirror in the house, Charlie's shaving mirror. Avelle applied a dash of lipstick, and a smidgen, (just a smidgen), of her Christmas perfume that Forrey had sent from San Francisco just before he shipped for Korea.

Avelle closed her eyes and spoke softly in her heart, "Oh Forrey, I am going to miss you. I won't ever forget you. I won't let my kids and Charlie forget, either. I'll talk about you every chance I get, and tell them what marvelous times we had when we were kids." The tears came closer to the surface again. Avelle stopped them before they took form. She scolded herself about how finally her face was back to normal and no longer did she have a headache.

Reluctantly, she knew it was time to get to her family. Avelle closed the door but didn't lock it. There was no need to lock any door in this small friendly town, full of nice neighbors like the Warnicks. She ought to stop and thank them on her way over to her folks. They were awfully nice to her yesterday. All the extra things neighbors do in times of trouble, just like being there when she got the phone call. Maud was a true friend, always ready to listen, always sharing hot rolls or fresh fruit. Avelle really liked Frank the best, though, poor gruff Frank. He never got a word in edgewise at home and he acted sometimes like he had almost given up speech altogether.

Avelle never seemed to enjoy friendships with girls and had never had a best friend. She seldom favored the little dainty things of girls, but instead enjoyed games the boys played as well as being outside. But Maud was different, somehow. She was like the mother Avelle had lost so long ago or an aunt, not like Aunt Nell, but a real aunt like other girls had.

Standing next door at the Warnick's, she knocked. Avelle was conscious that when the door opened, she was re-entering the world. A world that was stranger and harder where words like Taipei, Seoul, and Panmunjom, that no one ever heard of before, suddenly became part of the everyday language. A world where a boy from a little town in Idaho could become a twisted, burned corpse on a field half a world away. A world where the beloved brother you had assumed would always be around said goodbye one day was never again to be seen. Avelle watched the newsreels; the grotesque bodies that once were men inextricably mingled with the contorted machines and the wrenched earth that was once homes. No doubt the Koreans were as proud of their homes as she was of hers and they felt the same indefinable thrill at the idea of homeland. For the first time, she thought of them as citizens and parents, instead of a foreign race. Avelle felt closer to them.

War and grief were no longer read about in a school textbook or in a newspaper or newsreel. The man lost on a field half a world away was her brother. Little did she care for the reason of war. Maybe, she would find a clear political conviction after this awful sting of loss had subsided...maybe. To find a way to understand why her government would get involved with a place she had never known or ever cared to know...but not today, not now! Today she would see a sister holding the mangled body of a beloved brother.

Still standing at the closed door, Avelle wondered if they didn't hear her knock, because it sure was taking Maud a long time to answer the door. Raising her hand to knock again, the door opened and Charlie came out, followed by Frank and Maud, who stopped in the doorway. Amused at her astonished expression, they all laughed.

Maud began chattering, familiar and expected. "Charlie here, he said you'd want to come on in, and dinner's all ready and waitin' at the O'Brien's. He said you'd get to gabbin' and he'd never get you to leave! Land's sakes! I guess no man's gonna stand around and tell you you can't step into my house a minute if you're a mind to! I was tellin' him, 'now you looka here, Mr. Charlie...'"

Charlie interrupted Maud and smiled, "No, Princess, it's your Aunt Nell. She's fixed chicken and dumplings, and the kids were already eating when I left. I was supposed to get you and come right back. They'll think I'm a fine one, they will! But I just thought I'd stop a minute and thank Frank and Mrs. Warnick, here, for everything they've done."

"Oh, drop that stuff, now, Charlie, you hear? We were mighty glad to be of any help in time of trouble. That's what friends and neighbors are for, I always say."

Frank stood embarrassed and broke off a stem of the rosebush by the door, using it to clean the dottle out of his pipe and letting it fall into the flower bed, earning a venomous look from Maud, which he pretended not to see.

Avelle found her voice at last, and though it was husky from her prolonged weeping, it had a curiously child-like inflection with a hint of laughter never very far off.

"Well, I must say, you don't look much like Maud, Charlie! That's what I thought when you opened the door. 'My, Maud sure has changed since the last time I saw her.'"

Reluctant to touch upon the events of the last few days, an uneasy silence fell among the four. Frank cleared his throat, and they all spoke together.

"Well, Princess, they'll think we fell in."

"I was saying to Frank, just now..."

"Charlie, did you think you'd..."

The chorus broke with Avelle saying, "Maud, I've been meaning to ask you to help me with that pattern for Kath's sun-dress. It just don't seem to come out right no matter what I do. I'll bring it over if that's okay with you?"

"Of course its okay with me, you just bring it over just as soon as you can."

Charlie, mindful of the hour, interrupted the two before the conversation would force them back inside. "We just got to get on over to your folks, Princess, and besides I'm hungry, if you're not! I feel like I could eat the south end of an old gray horse."

Frank touched her arm, with a sense of commiseration. "That's a good idea, all right, Avelle. What you need about now is a good hot meal under your belt. It warms the inner man or woman. I suppose it's the same in both cases."

Avelle agreed with a sigh though her body was a little reluctant to move in any one direction. Charlie took her limp hand and escorted her away with several goodbyes. Charlie and Avelle walked across the highway toward her folk's house. Frank strolled off around the house on one of his interminable errands. Maud, scolded the absent Frank while cleaning the pipe residue out of her flower bed.

"How is everyone holding up?" Avelle wanted to be prepared when she walked into the home where the chaos of twelve growing children resided.

"I know the older ones have been shaken up a bit. But with the bustle of that clan, it's a wonder you can even hold on to one thought for longer than five seconds." Charlie and Avelle exchanged a quiet laugh.

Nell Beckman married Forrey and Avelle's father, Clarence, right after their mother died from cancer. Twelve children were born from that union, half of them being twins, although not one twin was identical. Nora and Dora were first, with blonde hair and blue eyes, and wore each other's clothes interchangeably and amicably. Dora teased Nora to the point of cruelty now and then, but still got on better than their twin brothers. Next were Timmy and Jimmy, ten months younger, full of fight and vinegar for each other. Timmy was big and blonde while Jimmy was slender with jet-black hair. The next four children were not twins, but barely fifteen months apart each; Vince, Margy, Connie, and Arlene. Nell had a three year pregnancy break before twins again, a boy and a girl, Freddie and Fay. Then another single birth with Teddy and the last born was Jody. Jody was a twin to start, but his twin brother never drew breath. Adorable, spoiled-rotten Jody, only five days older than Avelle's oldest was Kath.

# CHAPTER 2

THE USUAL MAD CONFUSION greeted the young couple at the O'Brien's; minus Vince, who was working for a farmer for the summer, and Margy and Connie who had elected to stay in town at the Vogler's until the unpleasantness at home abated somewhat. Nora was in tears over something rude that Dora had just said. Jimmy was sitting at the table flipping bread pellets at the smaller children who sat in a circle on the floor around the record player, which screamed the maniacal laughter of Woody Woodpecker at full volume. Aunt Nell, busily clearing away the children's table, was constantly being stopped because Timmy, not acting his age, would untie her apron strings as fast as she re-tied them. Papa was eating away, oblivious to all. Charlie and Avelle created a minor flurry as they came in, letting half a dozen fat flies out the tattered screen door, as if it mattered. The little ones who sat at the player, ran to Avelle, throwing fervent arms around whichever part of her anatomy they were able to reach. Kath reached Avelle first and searched her mother's face. Reassured by whatever she saw there she said her mommy looked very nice. Charlie, exasperated, turned the record player off, everyone's voices sounding strident in the ensuing contrast, and Freddie and Fay running right after to turn it back on.

"Go on, all of you, clear out of here!" said the voice of authority. "Get upstairs and clean up you four if you are going to the show. Shut off that screaming juke-box. My word! Mind now, or I'll tan you good! Arlene, you can take Kath and Chuckie over to see Emmy Lou's new kittens, if you'd like. Go on! Scat! My word!"

"Yes, Mom. And Mom, we'll need some money," Nora said, then kissed Avelle and drifted dreamily over and leaned on the door frame hoping to catch a quick glimpse of Dora's friend of the evening. As luck would have it, he pulled up to the curb in that very minute and Dora waved a careless good-bye, glared at Nora with a look that said more of her snoopiness and would without doubt be discussed in the morning, and vanished. Nora, still trying to get a look at the young man in the Thunderbird, put on speed and dashed into the front room to peer through the curtains kneeling on the davenport in full sight of the street, really earning the post-mortem reprimand.

Once they were out of sight, Nora drifted back into the huge old kitchen, again kissed Avelle, and dreamily said,

"Wow! Did you see that! I don't know how Miss Priss does it, really I don't! Handsome as Rock Hudson, and driving a 'Bird, to boot! Ah well, I don't live right, that much at least is obvious!" Nora drifted away up the stairs looking as ethereal as an angel, considering whether her blue dress was too soiled to wear once more. She murmured to herself, "Who cares, I'm only going to the show with my brothers."

As the hot kitchen quieted, Papa looked up from his plate and waved his fork motioning the young couple to him.

"Sit right down here and dig in, kids. Nell will have a spot cleaned off in just a minute there. Hungry, hey? Well, I'll have to say one thing for the old lady; she can sure cook when she puts her mind to it! These dumplins'll fill up that hole under your belt, and it won't take till tomorrow either." Clarence returned to his plate again with nothing else to say.

"I'm so sorry to have fiddled around until all of you are finished," Avelle apologized. "You hadn't ought to feed us at all. And Charlie is no better. Did he come get me, like you asked him to? No, he was talking to Frank and Maud, and I started over...well, I guess I stopped to talk to them too, to thank them...you know, they've been so nice to me...I mean, of course they would be...but you know..." her voice got sadder and sadder, and slower and slower, finally ceasing altogether. A tear wound slowly down her cheek.

"Aw, now, Princess, don't. Don't start in again. You're going to make yourself sick," Charlie gently pleaded.

Avelle, who had taken up her baby intently watched Aunt Nell's efficient clearing of the table, and sank gratefully into a chair. How did she do it with that rowdy tribe under

23

her feet all the time? It brought a tender smile to Avelle's eyes.

Nell silently and quickly slipped plates, silver and paper napkins into places and instinctively took tiny Nancy-Ann out of Avelle's arms. Sitting down at the side of her still eating husband, she sighed, wiped a mousy hair out of her eyes and poured coffee all around, seemingly all in one motion.

"Now, you kids start right in. I think the chicken and dumplings are still warm." Nell nervously encouraged her guests to eat. "Yes. Why, my word, you must be about starved. Avelle, dear, Charlie said you hadn't eaten a bite all day. Seems good to have this time with you now the others are finished. They do make so much noise!"

The food was good, and Avelle found herself unexpectedly hungry. She ate right on as Nora and her twin brothers came in for show money, slick and amazingly handsome. Bantering and shoving like two beaus competing for a sweet girl's attention, they climbed into the broken-down old car Forrey had left for them in common when he enlisted.

Arlene, who had gone over the alley to Emma Lou's with the younger ones, came to show Avelle an adorable kitten. Pets were a novelty to the O'Brien home, Aunt Nell logically forbade them on the grounds that a house with twelve children, Clarence O'Brien and herself was quite full enough.

The kitten's eyes had just opened, and its helplessness went to Avelle's heart. She stopped eating to take it and the baby set up a cry to "See. See." So she played with the cat and the chubby baby until Arlene, finding herself no longer the holder of the cat, left.

"Well, I think I'll just step over to the service station, see what was on the late news," said Papa, tilting back in his chair. Baffled by the lack of comment from his wife, who usually fought to delay him from continually leaving, Clarence said "Well...well," a couple of times, got up and left. No sooner had his footsteps receded than she rose and shut the door, cutting off the last rays of the June sunset outside.

Thus deprived of the last rays of natural light the room became quite dark. Aunt Nell rose again and lit a kerosene lamp then set it on the disorderly table. Avelle, not understanding her actions, rose up and began to clear the table.

"No, no. Don't bother with that, the twins are supposed to straighten everything up when they get back from the show. To pay for their tickets, you know. Won't hurt things a bit to sit."

"Now, I wanted to talk to you two a bit, if I could manage to get you aside for a minute. That is, if you feel up to a talk?" Nell paused for Avelle's affirmative nod. "I feel like it's important, and it ought to be settled right away. Just as soon as you feel up to talking it over, that is. Did Forrey say anything to you about his...well, his...insurance money?" She misinterpreted Avelle's stricken look and hastily continued, "It's not right, I know, to talk money so soon. But if you can give me some advice before...before your father..." she bogged down again, unable to criticize Clarence O'Brien to his beloved daughter, meek and a step-mother, and by nature always unsure of herself.

"I should have known this would come up sooner or later," Avelle thought, giving Charlie such a look. Her still sorrowed eyes gave her a different appearance. The little nod and smile Charlie gave, heartened her. She almost forgot the stabbing realization that she hadn't thought of Forrey all through dinner.

# CHAPTER 3

FORREST O'BRIEN WAS REFERRED to as "Forrey." If someone new to the community called him Forrest, they would have been immediately corrected with a, "Oh, you mean Forrey." He was the first born from his father's first marriage. He was tall and handsome with creamy smooth skin, dark wavy, almost curly hair, that when the sun shone just right would reveal a touch of red and green eyes that made the girls melt and swoon over him something awful. He was good-natured and well liked, but when his friends went out to "play mischief," Forrey was off fixing anything broken.

From Forrey's early adolescence, one could most likely find him at Mr. Max's garage. From his earliest years, Forrey had a knack for fixing things. Some even said, "It was a gift," like the gifted hand of a gardener that can make a fern grow in high desert soil. In Mr. Max's garage, Forrey found a place where he could hone his talent and help out financially at home. He was indeed an excellent mechanic, and soon the children who had brought Forrey their broken toys were now bringing him their broken vehicles. Mr. Max's business thrived with Forrey's reputation. The grandfatherly owner who had in the early years given Forrey simple chores to do out of sympathy took a quick notice to Forrey's natural abilities.

Mr. Max had no children of his own to pass the business on to, and Forrey had become like his own son. There could be no surprise that Mr. Max began making preparations to hand the garage over to Forrey. But the time had come in Forrey's life to answer his country's call which postponed any plans to setting down roots of his own.

Forrey had but one task on his leave that was unavoidable...to talk to his sister. With a sense of duty to his family, he knew they would have to talk about the one event that no one wants or expects. It was the topic of loss and pain, and the topic itself implicitly declared that death is a guaranteed fact. The fearful assumption is that making out a will or confronting the subject of mortality somehow permits your own demise or the demise of a loved one. It's as if to welcome the grim reaper to come at that very minute and steal like a thief the life still yet to be enjoyed.

Forrey knew Avelle would protest talking about it, or try everything she could to avoid it all together. His orders came in to be sent to North Korea. He would be sent to where bullets were piercing armor and piercing hearts. Unavoidably he must convey his intentions...here and now. Forrey felt that he could not count on ghost whispers in the dark when specific details and wishes were at such a high importance of being understood.

Avelle sat at the table remembering the last time she spoke with her brother. He was under the hood of Charlie's old Chevy. It was where Forrey was the most comfortable, the most at home. Charlie had said that the distributor, or points, or some other exotic-sounding malady had afflicted his Jalopy. So that Thursday morning in August before he would leave for war, he went to see what he could do with "the old rat-trap" while he waited until Avelle's morning chores were done.

Forrey kept looking up from under the hood while his sister washed with her old wringer Maytag Charlie's work clothes, mop rags, and cloths secured with wooden pins on the line, drying crisp and clean within the hour from the high desert August air. Avelle looked forward to the day when their savings would buy them their own house and a new electric Maytag washer. Kath was in the yard occupied in the duty of being a hostess at her tea party while Chuckie was trying to fix his trucks in the dirt like his Uncle Forrey, but with no success.

"Hey, Sis! You got a coke in that ice box of yours?"

Glad to be through with the drudge of the laborious chore, and eager for a chance to tease Forrey a little, she ran to him with a chilled coke all breathless and laughing.

"I'm not so parched you couldn't have walked it over,

Funny Face."

"I know, but I have missed you so much, and every second is precious." Avelle dropped herself down on a pile of old discarded railroad ties. "Boy, am I glad to be through with that job for a week."

"Blue Monday comes on Thursday this week, huh?" Forrey used the grill as leverage to pop off the cap. With one smooth effortless stroke, the cap flew off and he took his satisfying first sip. Closing the hood, Forrey perched himself on top of the Jalopy like a king upon his throne.

"I guess for lunch, I'll..."

"Sis, I need to talk something over with you. I guess I should by rights wait for Charlie and talk with you both, but I know whatever is right by you is okay with him, the big lug. I never saw a guy so crazy about a woman, just the same as from the first day he saw you. Makes us old bachelor types half sick to our stomachs. But this is nothing to do about love or marriage, and I don't want to get sidetracked either. This is important!"

Forrey's tone brought Avelle straight up to attention. It's not like her brother was never serious, but when he was serious, there was always good reason to pay attention. Avelle gave a slight nod to show her full attention and Forrey did his best to stay on track with his purpose.

"Well, Sis, it's like this. The way I see it, I got this GI insurance when I went in, and I put it in Kath and Chuckie's names. I would have put it to Mrs. Charles D. Brehan, but as I see it, she is pretty well set."

His smirk put a smile on her face and only nodded to

continue.

"But while I've been home this time, I've kind of had a change of mind you might say. This is the last leave I got before I go overseas, or wherever they send me, and as hot as things are in Korea now, that's where I'll be sent."

Avelle's attentive eyes welled up in surprise of what her beloved brother was insinuating.

"No. Now, don't get to getting all shook up, there's worse yet to come. If you stop me now from telling you my plan, who knows when I will ever have another chance like this to talk things over with you! I've pretty near given up already and asked you for an appointment." Avelle forced her wet eyes to dry.

"Thank you. Now, you know as well as I do that some of the guys that go over aren't coming back. Come on, Sis, bear with me. That's the worst of it." Avelle turned her icy gaze to the highway. No car passed from either direction as if time itself had stopped. With a deep sigh, she resolved herself to hear her brother out.

"I can't finish until I put it up to you just my way. I need to know you understand my reasons and have you with me on this. I'm the mechanic. I'm not in the combat troop, so it ain't too likely I'll get it overseas anyway. If I do get it, then at least I've done something with my life and will be able to help around here as if I'd never gone. Whereas, if I got it here on the highway where it's ten times more apt to happen, it means nothing. Once you've had it, you're a long time dead, regardless of where it happens...regardless. The question is not the insurance itself but to give it to who?"

"Give it to whom. Owl-face!" Avelle teased her brother by impersonating a schoolmarm.

"Okay, whom, then...naaa...who, whom. Oh, I see why you called me 'Owl-face' and a double naaa to you, too!" Forrey stuck out his tongue and continued with his purpose. "But look here. Here's a next-of-kin who doesn't need the insurance pay off, and her two kids will likely also never be hurting much. Am I correct so far?"

Forrey barely noticed Avelle's nod as he carried on. "And all the time right under our own noses is someone who really needs the money, who had always needed more money than she's been able to lay hands on, who scrimps and saves and cuts corners. Who is always getting a rough deal she didn't ask for, and who isn't bitter about it and never would be. She has always been on the short end of life and has resigned herself to that life. Nor has it occurred to her that she could ever do something to make things go better for herself and all the rest of us. To her, it's always the other guy who comes out in the end. I've never seen her spend a penny foolishly, have you? No, it's always been figure and scrimp, manage and save for the rest of us. And all the time leaning over backwards not to make a distinction between you and me and her own."

Avelle straightened her back on the Railroad ties where she sat listening to her brother. She didn't like Forrey making their stepmother into some sort of saint of hardships.

"Now there I will have to disagree! You were gone to the garage so much, unless you were in school or goofing someplace, you'd be surprised the things that I saw that you missed. She very definitely made the distinction always in our favor! You'd of thought we were royalty or something and the rest of the kids only commoners, if not outright serfs. When I was younger I thought it was because we were older, but it was more, I believe. I think mother must have left quite the impression on her. It most certainly wasn't the O'Brien blood! I used to laugh at the fairy tales, especially Cinderella and Snow White. The experience I'd had with a 'cruel stepmother' sure didn't jive with the word or description I'd heard. Didn't you ever notice?"

"Yeah, now that you mention it, I always thought it was so funny. It's Charlie who calls you 'Princess' and Aunt Nell who acts as if she really believes it."

A soft shade of rose was beginning to form on Avelle's face, "I know it's great to know you're loved, but it's like I'm on a pedestal that I have no right to be on. They both need to have better sense. Besides, Charlie shouldn't be calling me that in public. But I guess it's too late for him to stop it now."

Forrey didn't press the issue. He was not finished, and the time needed to get it all out was precious.

"But as I was saying before I was so rudely interrupted..."

"Oh, gee, sorry. Your handmaiden awaiteth." Avelle gave an apologetic nod.

"My savings, that goes to your kids, present and future, that's not what I am talking about. It's the GI insurance that is the big deal...the real money. Now I don't like to knock the Old Man, and I don't know what you and Charlie think," Forrey held out his hand to stop his sister. "No, dear, don't interrupt, because really...I don't want or care to know. It's just, well, I've given him money from time to time, and sooner or later I'd get around to checking and never once did he use it for what he said he wanted it for in the first place. It all went down the drain, or should I say 'down the hatch' that I finally got a little leery."

"Oh, Forrey, you shouldn't have!" Avelle would not allow Forrey to keep her silent on this point. "Do you know he used to ask me? Only I never had any. And last year I found out what went with Charlie's pocket money, and you better believe I put my foot down on that right away. One day I came in and he wasn't 'into' Kath's piggy-bank, but he just kind of laughed sick-like and said it was already getting so heavy, he wouldn't put anything in right then." Avelle glanced at her daughter still occupied with the tea party.

"Poor old drunk. I suppose he can't help it. I don't think I would quite mind it so much if it were anything but booze. Drugs would be so much worse. The point is what's to happen to Aunt Nell and the kids if I don't come back safe and sound? The two oldest twins are able to start taking care of themselves."

"I knew, of course, that you have your allotment check made out to Aunt Nell, is that what gave you the idea?"

"I think the idea was always there, The old man's history is what got it all started cuz I sure wasn't gonna put it in *his* name." Forrey looked up at a cloudless sky, praying for help not to judge his father too harshly.

"You know, I think he pretty much bums from just about everybody. I know he's hit Fred Warnick up often. I asked Frank about it, and of course he wouldn't tell. Maud admitted it, though, when I got right down and asked her. You wouldn't think I would have a hard time getting it out of her, but it was like she was covering for him or something. But I pointed out to her that it wasn't really a favor. As sure as God made little green apples, one of these days he'll drink himself to death unless he eases off. That day may not be as far off as you may think."

# CHAPTER 4

THE IRISH EYES OF this sister and brother stopped for a minute and were prone to find the sweetness of life and remember the good times.

"He didn't always used to be this way, did he Forrey? Seems like I remember when Mama was alive he was so different."

"No, I can't say he did, not much anyway. I think he was scared of Mama. It seems I remember when she was quite sick I heard her speak to him real sharp one day, and he acted like a whipped pup. But these past few years he seems to be really going downhill. Can you remember the good times before Mama died?"

"Not really remember. I mean I kind of have a vague feeling that someone who loved me was sick in bed, and everyone was busy and acted scared. I remember being set up on her bed and being scared, too. I remember the Fredrickson kids who lived where Warnicks do now. Molly broke my doll, and you know I have never had any use for her since."

"So that's what happened! We all wondered, and I know Aunt Nell was afraid you resented Molly for having a mother when you had just lost yours."

"I have never 'resented' Aunt Nell for taking Mama's place. I never thought of Mama as having a 'place' for Aunt Nell to take. She asked me one time when I was a teenager. I suppose I'd been snootier than usual. 'Resent...' 'replace...' these are words that don't fit, but neither does 'daughterly love.' Aunt Nell has never let me get that close. She doesn't love her own kids like that either, for that matter. But you'll have to admit, Aunt Nell always acts like somebody's servant."

"Well, she may have some kind of inborn servant psychosis, but it's probably the start she got. Did it ever occur to you that when Nora and Dora were born, she and Papa were only married five months?" Forrey stirred up their family's past hoping Avelle would truly understand why he wanted to change his beneficiary status.

"It never did occur to me until you just said it, but you're right. I knew she was keeping house for us when Mama died. I guess I just supposed Papa fell in love or else he turned to her for consolation after losing Mama. Ulk, how yuck! Whatever possessed her, let alone him?"

"Well, I suppose she got trapped into it. She never had

a break in her life, and it's just one more example of the kind of luck she's had from the beginning. From what I gathered she and her parents weren't in town very long when her father left...just abandoned them I guess. I remember he showed up one day when I was about ten or so and wanted money. That was during the false recovery from the depression, during Roosevelt's first term as President. It sure didn't take the old man long to send him packing. I remember that we were just ready to sit down to supper, and Aunt Nell cried because Papa wouldn't even let him stay to eat.

Aunt Nell was wiping her eyes and said, 'You told me to feed every bum that comes to the door, but that doesn't apply to my own father, I suppose.'

And Papa said, 'No, I can't say it does. A guy bummin' around looking for work is one thing, but that old reprobate is not an honest bum, he's an out-and-out deadbeat. And why you should want to feed him after the way he treated you and your mother and all is too much for me.' He slammed out of the house and didn't eat either."

Avelle looked down at the rocky driveway, saddened by her father's accusation of a man that some people in town now said about Clarence. "Did he honestly say that? Oh, Forrey, I don't think I will ever understand him."

"Well as I was saying, the townspeople fed them and took them in, but it wasn't long till Aunt Nell's own mother died. After that, she was moved around from pillar to post to help out with cooking and cleaning. Then it finally ended up in what looked to her like a good set-up, with the old man and us kids and a dying woman. I know for a fact he paid her wages, probably the first she ever got, which were a whole ten dollars a month not including her keep."

"Ten dollars a month?! How could he afford such a princely sum as all that?" Avelle rolled her eyes and scoffed.

"You need to remember that this was in the depression. Top-flight men were literally begging for work at a dollar a day and not finding it. So the job of keeping house for him and us, plus tending to Mama in the last days, looked pretty good to her, I imagine. What drove Papa to get her into his bed, I'll never know. The whole thing makes me sick to my stomach. But if I were to ever find out he was underhanded about it and used Aunt Nell, I'll punch his lights out."

"I know Charlie would second your sentiments. But how would a person ever know? It's not really the sort of question you can ask."

"It would be just one more hurt for her and one more event to be ashamed of, especially if we even gave the hint that we knew beyond the simple idea that's been swept under the rug."

"Do you think Mama knew? Besides, didn't Aunt Nell have a baby with her at first?"

"Yeah, but I don't think Mama knew. Or at least I pray that she was too sick to notice. I think Aunt Nell hid it from everyone, including herself. Ignore what you're doing is wrong and somehow it's not so bad, I suppose. Right after Mama died, I think she spilled the beans to Mrs. Fredrickson, and Mrs. Fredrickson went to Papa and insisted on him 'doing the right thing by our Nell!'"

"You would think they were in love with all the kids they went on to have."

"Odd isn't it? It's not like either one of them act like they love each other. It's more like they tolerate each other. Did you ever see Cheaper by the Dozen?"

"Yes, and it didn't strike me as particularly funny either. It was a home cooked up and romanticized. It may have been funny or even fun to someone who didn't live with it day in and day out."

Forrey, finding himself completely off the topic he had once started, jumped off the hood to look at the motor once again for some advice on how to finish what he had started. But also he was enjoying this conversation with his sister; he didn't want any of it to end. Avelle was also enjoying her brother's company. Rising from the Railroad ties, Avelle walked over to the side of the Jalopy.

Forrey had explained the principles of internal combustion to her for as long as she could remember, and yet she never got in a car to go someplace without feeling as though a miracle was happening when the cold metal came to life and started moving forward. It always seemed to her like some kind of black magic spell was on the key when it turned to roar the engine to life. One would think that at some point the genius Forrey had with motors would have rubbed off, but she peered into the inner workings of the Jalopy with absolutely no comprehension.

Twisting a ratchet in his hand, Forrey turned his back on the Jalopy and spoke with contemplation. "You know, it wasn't until I got old enough to have feelings for girls myself that I cut the old man some slack. I mean think about it. He's got a dying wife whom he adores, two little kids, and although not a striking beauty, at least a decent looking young woman in his house day and night. Stranger and more unwelcoming circumstances have brought people together before, I suppose."

"Honestly, brother dear, I would rather not think about any of this. Anyway, I thought you were maybe practicing up to become a monk or something. I didn't know you were interested in girls!" Avelle nudged her shoulder into her brother's arm.

"I do...or at least did until you spoiled the whole set-up for me!"

"Me? Why? I never said a word to you about a girl in my life! You never went with one long enough for me to get to know their names, let alone tease you about one of them."

"Yeah, I know. About the time I'd almost get interested, I'd get around you and Charlie, and I would compare what she and I had going with what you and Charlie had for each other and I just couldn't see that much in it for me. I don't think I've got it in me to love any woman like he loves you, Sis. With me, wheels come first, and women come in a poor second; whereas, you know very well he thinks the sun and moon rises and sets because you say so."

Forrey looked at the clothes silently drying on the line while his niece and nephew remained engrossed in their play.

"That is sweet of you to say, but you shouldn't judge your love for a girl by Charlie. And certainly don't put us up on a pedestal where we don't belong. Too often people make marriage a convenience, and don't give themselves a chance to really love each other. Just you wait, my dear brother! When that girl does finally come knocking at your door, wheels will come in a poor second to her."

"I doubt it, but we'll see. Anyway, what I wanted to say about Aunt Nell and the kids, before we got sidetracked, is what will they do for money? I don't see how they are going to make out. I didn't realize that my financial contribution was all that was keeping a roof over their heads and food in the cupboards. I know the GI insurance was made out to Kath and Chuckie, but I need to consider those in our family who got nothing' without it. And I am making it out so Papa can't just take it to booze up on."

"I think that's wonderful of you, Forrey! Charlie said just the other day he didn't see how they were getting along with you gone. He said you probably didn't do them any favor handing out so much of your wages when you were home, but if you hadn't of done it, Papa would have been obliged to get some sort of job. I think the allotment will be a Godsend, the very thing. But I would rather have you home safe and sound, and so would they."

"I don't know why I didn't think of it sooner. I've kind of felt a little cut loose from them since I enlisted. I know that this year is going to be more expensive with the girls graduating and all. That's why I want the money to go for the kids. It's really not about Aunt Nell or Papa either for that matter. Those kids didn't ask for the life they got, and that's who I'm thinking about. That is, unless you and

Charlie think your kids should have it. It's them that should have the right to it. I know I should wait till Charlie is here to bring it up, but I never seem to get around to saying anything to him, and my leave is slipping away."

"I don't know why my kids are more 'entitled' to it than anyone else. I just hope and pray nobody gets it at all!"

"Oh, I don't expect they will, and I sure don't think I'm the irreplaceable man either. But as for the brood, I can't see where the money they need will come from unless I supply it. If I thought for a minute Papa would supply it...which means he would have to straighten himself up...and I don't see any signs of that happening...I wouldn't be having this conversation with you. This is not the kind of thing you look forward to just because it would come in handy. Still, you talk it over with Charlie, and I won't do it if you don't think I should."

"I don't have to wait to see what Charlie thinks, thanks just the same. I think it's wonderful of you to be thinking of them. Besides I know for sure he wouldn't want your insurance for our kids. He loves you too much, as I do, and it would seem like blood money to him the same as it would to me. He's told me a dozen times he thinks more of you than of any brother he's got. You know how he's been since you've been here. Honestly, the two of you make me so mad! You're worse to sit and talk than a couple of old women!"

"I figured as much. But I want to make sure you understand that my savings goes to your kids. No protesting...I mean it! The rest of my things...the wardrobe, the bookcase I made, my tools...they're all Charlie's. That's why I left him here in the first place."

Avelle just stood looking at her brother soaking every facet of his face and manner and yet boiling the Irish blood in her for him talking this way, talking like this was the last time he would be home. Putting his will out to her like this, as if the minute he touched North Korean soil he would be dead.

"Sis, I know this isn't the kind of thing you talk about, but I had to get it off my chest. Don't look at me like that! It's not like I'm asking to die, nor do I expect to. I just have to have it in order. Please try to understand."

Avelle leaped into his arms and held him tightly. "I understand. Just get home okay!"

"Okay. Now what's for lunch? Just because its wash day doesn't mean you can starve me flat."

"Good grief! Kath and Chuckie must be starving, too, unless Maud fed them already. She's always giving them something. I swear! Maud spoils them awful." Avelle snatched up the pink plastic lined bushel basket and hurried toward the house, calling her children inside.

Forrey watched his sister call out to her children to pick up their toys before lunch and go inside the house. She reminded him of their mother, full of life and spirit, independent and free, but loving, loyal and devoted to her husband and children, as well as the rest of her family. They shared the same hair color, but Avelle's eyes were browner like her mother's, and her skin was fairer than his. In his heart, no woman could hold a candle to his sister, though he would never tell her that.

Forrey playfully washed up with his niece and nephew while Avelle prepared lunch. He had pretty much said all he needed to say, but hoped that after lunch and with the kids back off to play, the two could sit down for some more soul talk.

With lunch over, Avelle wanted to talk more about the demise of their mother. She was amazed and impressed at how much Forrey remembered with only being a couple years older than she.

"Wasn't Mama sick a long time before we lost her? It seems like I only remember her being in a great high, hard bed."

"Not really long when it comes to years, but long as it comes to months. It seems as though it was almost a year. I'm pretty sure she was home about the time Papa got cut back to three days a week. That would have been October of 1933. She was in the hospital only a few weeks. The depression was really taking a toll and the sections were cut back to three days a week. Papa thought he could take care of her himself, with a little help from the neighbors. He soon found out it's no snap for a man to keep house with a couple of little kids, let alone a dying wife. He did end up getting a hospital bed through some charity, and that made it a little easier for Mama. I guess you can easily see why he got Aunt Nell to come and work for us."

"But he didn't drink much in those days, did he? Seems like I remember one Fourth of July he drank too much and it was an item of comment for quite awhile."

"I don't really remember that. I know he never drank to any excess while the older twins were little. But it seems that after they all kept coming, and he had lost his job here on the section, he began going to the bottle more and more. I guess he just got discouraged, though I don't doubt he loves them all."

"Yes, including us. It's not Papa that makes the distinction, it's Aunt Nell."

"Well yes, that's true. It just seems to me that he's given up trying, and he doesn't seem to care or even try to straighten himself up."

Avelle was grateful that her brother stopped talking for a moment. She had so much to process, to take in everything Forrey had been saying that morning.

"Want some lemonade? Robertson's market had fresh lemons the other day."

"Wow, I'm getting quite the kingly treatment today."

"Oh, don't be coy."

Forrey peacefully smiled as he sat stretched out on the kitchen chair. Avelle prepared her lemonade in the very same kitchen when they were the children of the Section Foreman. The memories that lay in the recesses of the minds of both brother and sister sprinkled in like the sunshine revealing dust through a window.

# CHAPTER 5

AS FAR BACK AS they could remember about Railroad history, there were three different companies spread throughout the lower forty-eight states. Each company was distinctively marked with its own colors: the Northern Pacific was blue-green, the Southern Pacific was red, and the Union Pacific was yellow with brown trim. For the most part, how a track was laid or how a locomotive roared to life and traveled or stopped on the tracks or many of the other basic functions were elementary to the three different Railroad companies.

Those living in Railroad Row at King Hill, Idaho, were in the heart of the Union Pacific Railroad. Clarence O'Brien was Section Foreman in the Maintenance of Way Department. The sections of this Department were divided up in mileposts of the Railroad tracks that each section crew was given to maintain in an eight-hour work shift. The section crew positions were highly coveted because they would be home every evening and never had to worry about being moved around from pillar to post within the company. All the more was the coveted position of Section Foreman. He was given a home in Railroad Row rent free for as long as he held his job. He could easily live there, raise a family and never move until he retired.

The job of the Section Foreman was to replace rails and ties that were damaged by the train. If the Locomotive had been started too quickly by the Engineer, or if the train would have to make an emergency stop, it would cut up the rails like Mores code and be rough for the next train that would come upon them. If the rough patch of rail was neglected or a tie too loose from the rail, it was sure to create a derailment. When an Engineer would come upon this rough track, he would have two choices: Call it in to the dispatch and start the chain of command to get it fixed, or take the Section Foreman to the side and speak to him personally. The latter is only done out of respect for the Foreman.

When a call is placed, the dispatch calls the Roadmaster, the Roadmaster calls the Inspector, and the Inspector inspects the track at the milepost called in. He then notifies the Foreman, and the Roadmaster reprimands the Foreman for not knowing his section well enough to have prematurely repaired the rail. It is the Section Foreman's job to telepathically see his section at every minute and to be able to feel the rails even in his sleep if any rail or tie is disturbed from its perfected beginning.

The Section Foremen were also a paternal lot. Besides the responsibility of their section of rails being in perfect order, and the authority to hire and fire, they also took it as their duty to see to the welfare and well being of their men. Their paychecks were entrusted to the Foreman, and if any of the crew were in a tight pinch between paydays, the Foreman would spot him and take care of it on payday. Many a Section Foreman stood as Godfather to a good few of his men's babies. Sometimes they were named after him or his wife.

Clarence O'Brien was not the worst Section Foreman the company had seen, but his luck at minor rules being broken were soon at an end, and his career was soon to be over. During the night, a freight train had left a car of ice containing several layers of blocks weighing 100-200 pounds. The train crew must have been in good humor and lined it up all nicely and neatly to the icehouse door. It always paid to be nice to the train crew because if you weren't, a cruel practical joke would be played on your crew and sweating swearing labor of moving the boxcar in line of the icehouse door would have to be done with pinch bars. It was Clarence's responsibility to set the schedule and pace of the work, to order the necessary supplies, and to see that each man performed his share of the work.

The icehouse was a partially sunken, double-walled structure of ties on the opposite side of the tracks from the houses on Railroad Row. Great care was taken to put in a requisition for plenty of ice before the weather turned hot, for in winter the Railroad right-of-way is colder than the Arctic's and in summer the cindered lane of steel is so hot the sweat coming off your nose is boiling before it hits the ground. It took about an hour for the crew to clean the icehouse, where over the winter the thawed and refrozen ice mixed with what was left of the sawdust and had now become a rotten, rubbishy, black, sticky, soup of slop. After breaking the seal on the boxcar, they cleared out enough sawdust to lay in the new ice. They set up the unloading chute built of heavy planking, which was stored from year to year outside on the roof of the icehouse. Within the boxcar, each layer and chunk of ice was separated by sawdust, to be transported by the chute into the icehouse and stored in the same manner as the boxcar.

Clarence had unwisely chosen to go to town the night before and had run into some old drinking buddies. That morning his head was in no condition to work, and with a weakened mind he had failed to inspect the condition of the chute. If he had been at work with a complete and sober mind he would have seen that one of the planks had been severely compromised during the year of storage.

The whole first layer of ice went in without mishap, and was covered with sawdust; however, the first block in the second layer had frozen to its neighbor and had broken off half as much, forming an unfriendly and lop-sided 300 pound chunk. It came off its sawdust reluctantly, and refused to slide down the chute. Had Clarence been on the watch, instead of daydreaming across town, his view would have seen that the men could have simply kicked it over the side. But as it was, one of the men kicked the ice to get it started down the chute. As it came down, it bucked and twisted and hit the fractured plank that gave momentum and thrust to turn again before it fell, echoing a mournful cry. With its sharpest edge down it faced one of the crewmen and screaming as if to suspend the fall with his cry, he was pinned to the ground. Not a man there could ever expect to pick him up alive. They were, however, smart enough to leave him where he fell, once they were able to get the ice off him. The Doctor commended them for that, once he had arrived there and looked over the situation. They closed the icehouse and the boxcar doors and waited for the Company Inspector. Nothing much else was done that day.

Clarence O'Brien from that day on would never work a regular day ever in his life again. It was not enough that he had broken several well known Rules; F- failure of adequate supplies, G-intoxication, L- being alert on duty, the worst of it was that he had broken Rule M- no care was exercised to avoid any injury to not only himself but others also. One of his men was dead because of his negligence. Clarence added to himself one more strike against himself. His children might never know how much loathing of himself he put into the bottle, but there was one who would make an effort to once again give him hope.

It seemed Aunt Nell had seen it coming, Clarence being fired for good, because before the Doctor had arrived on the scene, an old abandoned hotel was rented to the enlarging O'Brien brood. They would be completely moved out of the

Section House before the sun would set that day.

Now, almost twenty years later, Avelle was the wife and her husband Charlie (though not Section Foreman) was working on the very same section while waiting for the layoffs to end and to be able to begin his career of aspiring to become an Engineer.

# CHAPTER 6

"CARE TO JOIN ME on the stoop?" Avelle turned to face Forrey with a full glass of sweet fresh lemonade in each hand.

"Don't mind if I do, Sis."

Sitting down on the stoop, they had a clear view of the town. Across the highway was the town of King Hill, a town where the parents knew what their kids were doing even before they ever got home. A store was first in view with Mr. Max's garage across the street to the west. The rooming house with the post office attached lay behind the store. South behind the rooming house and across the street to the east was the old hotel that was still the home of the O'Brien clan.

"Well, even if the old man hadn't of gotten fired like he

did, they would have had to move us all anyway." Forrey looked back over his shoulder at the section house and mused, "Could you imagine sixteen people living in this place?"

Avelle broke out laughing and just about spilled her lemonade, "That certainly would be quite a sight, brother dear."

The rest of the afternoon the two siblings talked and reminisced and watched the two children play, refusing to let the day, or life as they knew it, end.

Now ten months later, Avelle sat treasuring that one last memory and forcing her mind to not forget one look, one feel, one wisp of air, or the color of the sky. For years to come, this one memory, this one summer, this one-week, would be able to be retold without contradiction to her grandchildren.

Nell would never forget when Avelle came storming into her home with a face as white as Marley's ghost and standing as stiff as a stone. Avelle was never known to speak all in one breath, but this time it was as if her rapid message was the only thing holding her together.

"Aunt Nell, I had to come right over. I had a phone call. It was the telegraph operator, Mr. Potter, in Glenns Ferry. He said that we had a telegram from the War Department. It was somebody called Mr. Potter from the Depot with a message. First he asked me if I was alone, and I told him no, Maud was here with me. He said that he was sorry and that he had bad news and wanted to know if I wanted to wait until Charlie was home to read it to me. I had a hunch, and there was no way I was going to leave myself in suspense. Besides, Charlie would be home anytime. He's still not home, and I got no idea how I'm going to tell him." Avelle took a deep breath as if gaining some courage and yet hoping the air would further suppress any sting of pain that was beginning to surface. "Anyway, I said no, and to go ahead. Mr. Potter said that the War Department wanted us to know that Forrey is DEAD!"

Nell fell to her chair as if the strength from her legs could no longer support her body. As Nell looked up at Avelle, it seemed that the next sentence made her step-daughter tower taller in her navy blue and green cotton checkered sun dress. "They said they were sorry and that he was a hero, 'Above and beyond the call of duty' I think is the way they put it. They said we should be proud....PROUD!"

Horror filled Nell's mind, "Oh what shall we do now! What's to become of us now?"

The two women painted quite the unusual scene. The young vibrant woman had her black hair with Irish red highlights combed perfectly, the ends flipped upwards just above the shoulders, still perfectly styled from the morning. The older woman had brown and grey hair matted in an attempted bun with strands going every direction they wished. Aunt Nell sat slumped over in her rocking chair, her soiled apron from the day's chores now holding her cries. The younger consoled her elder with caring hands upon sobbing shoulders. The burning tears of loss filled Avelle's eyes, and the dam that was never before given permission to break gushed from Nell's.

"Does your Father know yet?" Aunt Nell barely lifted her face from her apron.

"I have no idea. Forrey may have listed us both as next of kin, or only me. He didn't say, and I didn't ask. Charlie and I have already made plans to go into town tonight. Maud has the kids now, and I was already to go before I got the news."

"Oh, I just wish I didn't have to tell the kids, is all. This is going to just bust them up. How am I ever going to be able to tell them?" Aunt Nell dropped her face fully into her hands with her apron crunched and wrinkled as she wept with years of sorrows.

"You're just going to have to come right out with it. They all should be home soon anyway." Avelle's voice turned from the strong informer to a softer counselor, "We'll all have to try to help each other the best we can. Charlie will be home any minute. I'm sorry but I just can't stay."

Aunt Nell barely nodded, and Avelle dashed from the house as if fleeing from the bitter sorrow and tears mounting in her own eyes. Avelle began to walk briskly home with the sun's rays beaming down with intensity, as if the rays were beating down on the earth with every pound of Avelle's broken heart. But just as the stubborn summer days in Idaho will not allow rain to fall from the sky, Avelle would get through this day without shedding one tear for her brother.

Barely reaching the corner her face hit the chest of her husband. "Hey! Watch where you're walking, Princess."

The look on his face told her everything she needed to know. She would be spared having to tell him, and her one relief in this horrid day. They were the kindred spirits God had intended when on their wedding day the minister announced, "These two became one flesh."

"You okay? We can cancel our plans for tonight, if you want to." Charlie did not ask or demand they change their plans. His wife needed her space, and he knew if he forced her out of the shock she was in, her heart would never really heal.

"No! No! I don't feel right in breaking my appointment. Besides, we probably need to hunt down Papa. I'll ask Maud to watch the kids tonight."

Maud had all three Brehan children in the tub and had just washed their hair when Avelle and Charlie walked in the front door. Avelle went right to the pantry-turned-bathroom with a towel and started drying and dressing Kath as Maud started with Chuckie. Both children tore from being dressed and ran to their father with their traditional welcome home hug. Avelle, who had no energy to scold her two oldest for running to their father in nothing but their underwear, turned to her youngest to towel off and dress. Maud set herself to drain and clean the tub.

# CHAPTER 7

IN CHARLIE'S HEART, HIS wife held the sun and moon, but it was his angelic five-year-old daughter, his firstborn, who could melt his heart and make the sun shine on a cloudy day.

"Here's your slip, Honey, and your dress. My aren't you the fashion queen!" Charlie laughed to himself to think of what the guys at work would say if they knew how much he enjoyed helping out with his kids. "Here, give your old Dad another kiss. Careful not to get too close against my clothes, Kitten. I'll give you a big teddy bear hug when I get washed up."

"Daddy, I was scared when you came home before and didn't give us a kiss. Did you be mad because we weren't ready to go?"

"Oh, no, no, Peaches! We just had some bad news today, that's all, and I had to see Mommy right away."

"Bad news?" Both Kath and Chuckie looked at their father and then their mother, wondering if they should be afraid.

"Was somebody bad, Daddy?" Questioned Chuckie, hoping it wasn't him.

"No, nobody did anything bad. I promise we will talk about it later, but right now I need to get cleaned up, okay?"

"Okay," spoke the two in unison with softer voices and turned back to their mother to finish getting dressed.

Charlie had forgotten that Maud was still in the house when he headed for the pantry himself and began unbuttoning his grimy denim work shirt. He stepped back in dismay at the awareness that a different woman, not his wife, was preparing his bath. Maud turned and misinterpreted his look of surprise as a sign of inner turmoil. She threw her arms around him and gave him a kiss of condolence on his cheek. Heaven knows what she might have said because in that same moment they were interrupted by Frank bursting in from the porch.

"Hey, what's all this?! Not only do I come home with nothing but supper on my table, but when I get over here, she's kissin' and huggin' the neighbor. How 'bout that?" He threw his hands on his hips as if ready for a western duel. Maud flew out of the house grabbing Frank by the shirt collar, nearly dragging him to the ground. Not until they had gotten down the steps of the Brehan's porch was Frank able to find words again to speak.

"What is going on here? Maud, you better explain yourself here, you're actin' like a crazy woman!"

Maud simply kept walking to their house, pounding her feet into the ground as if to dare her husband to follow her expressively clear footprints. The minute Frank stepped inside their door, Maud was loaded with the paper in her hand and shoved it to his chest.

"There! That's what's the matter, you big boob! Just you read that! You'll see how smart you are! You and your big talk about kissin' on the neighbor!"

Like most couples the Warnick's had their share of marriage troubles too, but Frank knew that it was his turn to eat crow when Maud shoved the penciled scrawl proof into his hands.

*"Regret to inform you of the death...*
*brother Forrest F. O'Brien...*
*Hero's death...*
*wounds sustained in the performance of his duty...*
*finest tradition...*
*country's loss...*
*forever proud..."*

and some word he couldn't make out, probably the Officer's name in charge. In what seemed to be the exact center of the page was a welt where a big wet tear had fallen.

"When did you get this?" Frank could barely get the words out. Surprised that he was still standing up, he looked for a place to sit down.

"This afternoon." Without stopping for breath, as she was always prone to do, Maud related to Frank the details of the afternoon, whether he wanted them or not.

"I was visiting Avelle and right at a quarter to four, someone phoned and Avelle asked me to answer the phone on account of her being in the middle of changing the baby. It was someone from the Depot. He asked if I was a neighbor of Mrs. Charles Brehan. When I said, 'yes,' he said, 'could you summon her to the phone, or would I sooner wait till her husband got home, as it was a death message?' Well, I told him they were working a lot of overtime lately, and I didn't know if Charlie would get home right at quittin' time. And he wanted to know if I was close enough to her to stay with her when she got the message. And I told him, 'I reckon I'm about the best friend she had,' so he said to go ahead and get her. I knew what it was the minute he said it was a death message." Maud paused as if reflecting that there was more meaning in her next words. "So I went over and told her as easy as I knew how, and do you know Frank, she never shed a tear or anything. Her eyes just got big as anything, and all she said was, would I stay with the kids while she went over to tell Nell. Course I did, quick as a heartbeat, but before she got back, Charlie came in and wasn't he surprised to see me there and Avelle nowhere in sight!" Maud chuckled a little before she wrapped up her story. "So, soon as I told him, why he took right off to get her. And she ain't cried yet, poor little thing!" Tears began to spill over as she laid her head on her husband's shoulder.

"Now, now. That ain't gonna help a thing, Maud. What we got to do now is figure out the best way we can be of help. You know that. This ain't no time to be thinkin' of how bad we feel." Frank's eyes were beginning to spill a few tears, too, and for the moment they shared in the spirit of grief with their friends.

"Well, of course, that's what we gotta think of now. Now, let's see..." And as if Frank's small sentences were marching orders, Maud sniffed and snuffed her tears dry and embarked on a plan of action all of her own. "They was meanin' to go to town. Avelle had a few things to do, and she's got an appointment with the doctor, they were plannin' to eat at the cafe' and maybe a show. I suppose that's all off now. I don't think she knows if Clarence has been told or not and probably wants to go hunt him up. Maybe we ought to go back over there and see if they want to eat with us."

The only thing consistent about life in any Railroader company is that it is irregular and inconsistent. Nowhere is it truer than the tracks at Railroad Row. At irregular intervals trains clatter by, halting all attempts at conversation until the roaring clickity-clack interruption has passed. As Frank and Maud approached the front door, a freight train passed by silencing any knock that would have otherwise been heard. At about the time the sixtieth freight car was passing, Charlie glanced at the front door and saw the couple standing on the outside of the screen and waved for them to let themselves in. It was another couple of minutes until the train had passed that their conversation could begin.

Frank cleared his throat and began his apology. "Say, I uh, want to apologize about me stormin' in here and actin' a fool.

I hope you're not sore. Besides, I should have known better instead of opening my big mouth and bein' a smart-aleck."

"Why, that's all right. Don't think anymore about it. You couldn't have known before you were told." Charlie stuck out his hand to Frank and shook, sealing the apology and forgiveness without another word or thought.

Avelle came from the back bedroom where she had just finished with Kath and Nancy Ann's hair. "Were you here before, Frank? I must have been in the other room."

Frank seemed by instinct to not even try to formulate and answer for Avelle. Maud unfailingly cut to the quick with her exuberant invitation.

"Came over to invite you folks to supper. It ain't much, just ham hocks and turnip greens. But I do got some shortcake out of the last of the strawberries." Maud didn't understand her friend's icy calm, but was willing to play along.

"Oh, no thanks. I don't want to miss my appointment with the Doctor, and I need to hunt Papa up, too." Before Avelle could make out any other sentence or request, her eldest made her objection.

"Oh, Mama, Mama. I want to eat with Mrs. Maud tonight! I don't want to go to the doctor. You promised if I watched Chuckie and Nancy Ann and kept them away from the garden a whole week I could have the next thing I asked for. Please can we go and have shortcake with Mrs. Maud?"

"Me too, Mommy! Me too?" cried Chuckie. "Shorecake, my fravrite!"

"Me! Me!" Chimed Nancy Ann not wanting to be left

out.

"Well, how 'bout this?" Frank broke in, "Why not leave the kiddies with Maud, and I'll go to town with you, if that's all right. I have to get a haircut anyway."

"Or a dog license." Maud smirked.

"I was hoping you would offer, Maud, though I meant to ask you earlier. I really appreciate it."

"Okay, kids, looks like it's shortcake for the girls and boy who are good and eat their dinner." Maud took any moment she could with the Brehan children to be the mom she always wanted to be, but secretly enjoyed being spared the trials of motherhood.

"Say, Frank, do you mind driving? That Jalopy of mine has about had it, and Forrey's tinkering didn't help either." Charlie whipped his eyes to Avelle as if slapped across the face by his slip of the tongue.

"Sure thing!" Frank quickly added, trying to help his friend recover from his insensitivity.

Avelle, however, never did hear Charlie's slip above the children's grateful cries of, "Shortcake!" "Shorecake!" "Cake!" She did, however, glance over at their Preston wall clock in the hallway just as it was chiming the three-quarter hour. "Charlie, my appointment is in half an hour and I want to be a little early."

The total drive time from King Hill to the doctor's office in Glenns Ferry is under fifteen minutes, but every click of the second hand hurried them all into action. Frank had voiced his request on changing out of his work clothes; Avelle was busy getting the children situated for the evening with Maud. Charlie thought it best to phone Mr. Max, and Maud hurried to get the children to her table and eating and Avelle out of earshot of Charlie's phone conversation with Mr. Max.

Maud had a friend that was laid up with a broken hip in the back bedroom of the doctor's home, and wanted to send her a bouquet of her prize roses. The doctor had fitted up his large home as an emergency hospital, with his office in the front. Any serious medical ailments meant at the very least a thirty to seventy-mile trip to any of the regular hospitals, either traveling west to Mountain Home or Boise, or east to Twin Falls. The doctor had, with pride, planted a most welcoming garden of flowers. But Maud insisted that her roses would be the best medicine to cheer her, more so than all the variety of flowers she could see from her room's window.

Doc Harrison was an old bachelor, and good thing, too. With being the Company doctor as well as the doctor for the townspeople, he had no time for a regular domestic lifestyle. He was just as busy and as irregular as the train crews. His nurse was at her wits end to keep the patient schedule within confined days: Children and expectant mothers on Monday, workers on Tuesday and Thursday, chronic cases on Wednesday, with Friday being the only unregulated day. His nurse would constantly complain that every day was treated like a free-for-all because no one would pay the slightest attention to her ordered schedule.

With Avelle's arms filled with a newspaper cornucopia of roses, she and Charlie kissed their children good-bye and reminded them to behave. Frank got behind the wheel of his aqua-green DeSoto Club Coupe as Avelle slid into the middle, Charlie placed Maud's gift in the back, then took his place beside his wife. As the DeSoto purred to life, Avelle couldn't help but secretly agree to Charlie's intention of buying their first new car. They were building up their savings to buy a house without a mortgage, which meant making a lot of sacrifices and not buying many of the new things their friends were already buying.

"Do you want me to hunt up Clarence while you're at the doctor's, Princess?"

"Oh, Honey, no. You know I can't stand to sit there and wait for you to come back! Please won't you stay with me?"

Frank broke in before Charlie had a chance to assure her. "Well, I'll tell you what, why don't you drop me off at the barber's and you two take my car. You can go do your thing at the Doc's and hunt up your father. Do you want to meet me at that El Sombrero place in an hour?"

"Yeah, I had heard they turned it into a restaurant of some kind," Charlie grumbled and sarcastically rolled his eyes.

"Don't mind him, Frank. Charlie swore he'd never set foot in there. I think it sounds real nice." Avelle smirked at her husband.

"Why did you say that, Charlie?" asked Frank a little confused.

"Barry asked the rails not to eat there anymore."

Frank pulled himself up to the steering wheel in order to look squarer on Charlie. "You're kidding. Why did he go and say that for?"

"Said their dirty work clothes got the seats soiled and the travelers didn't like to get their 'finery in disarray.'" Charlie was still resentful for an owner not wanting to serve his co-workers.

"Oh, really?!" Frank straightened himself and acted out with supposed refinement "Well, La-De-Da!" As they neared closer to town Frank wasn't sure now if he wanted to go there himself.

"So, Barry asked the rails not to eat in there, huh? Most people would go out of their way to get the men over there. I mean, a Railroader will spend three times the money that any tourists could, not to mention the repeat business. Barry's crazy!"

`Charlie could tell Avelle was looking at him, reminding him of a certain possible reason. "Well, I have an idea it was the Roundhouse crew he was talkin' to at the time. They do get awful filthy."

Avelle couldn't help but add to what her husband said. "I happen to know personally that their wives have to send their clothes to the laundry. No regular washing machine could even begin to take that heavy grease and oil out."

All three of them began to feel that maybe Barry had a valid point, and like most small towns, the real reason got lost in the gossip.

It is an unspoken creed of the workers in the Company. If the lowest guy of the payroll isn't welcome somewhere, then no one is; however, Charlie couldn't help but give some sympathy to Barry's other patrons. "I guess I don't like it much either, to sit down where one of them's been, even if they spread a newspaper on the seat."

Frank was still trying to sort out the rumor in his mind. "Why would he object to the Trainmen? They're as clean as any man in dress clothes. Besides, they eat like kings orderin' those big steak dinners and lobster tails and such. You'll be one of those, too, and real soon from what I hear. Won't you, boy?"

Charlie knew that Frank couldn't help himself to tease a little; he also knew Frank had no appetite for the long hours and irregular schedule of the Trainmen.

"I don't remember who said it, but I am sure it was the Roundhouse bunch. If the Trainmen are the kings, then they're probably the serfs, on account that they don't spend much money."

"Yeah, I know." Frank didn't like degrading any man willing to work, but the Roundhouse crew was known for having a bad reputation. "Lately I've been half sore at them myself, too. Always pushin' and horsin' around all the while usin' filthy language without thinkin'. They've been known to sneak away for coffee, or even a beer, without wantin' to get back to work. I guess the Roundhouse Foreman is pretty hard up for help."

"Well, the turnover on most of those jobs is pretty high. Even though it's lousy work and lousy pay, doesn't make it right for a man not to be honest in his job." When Charlie saw that they were pulling up to the barbers, he was grateful the conversation was over.

Frank and Charlie got out of the DeSoto in unison, "You

know, we can meet somewhere other than El Sombrero?"

"No, actually I would prefer a quiet place tonight." With a watchful eye on Avelle, Charlie slipped in behind the wheel and within the next few blocks, pulled into the doctor's driveway.

# CHAPTER 8

AVELLE CAME OUT OF the examination room looking
pale and distraught, though she thought she was giving
Charlie a smile that said she was just fine. The doctor had
escorted her out and seated her in a comfortable chair. He
asked Charlie to step into his office. He closed his door as
Charlie took a seat and then began to lecture Charlie as he
leaned on the edge of his desk with arms crossed.

"See here, son, what have you been doing to that girl?
She's in a state of shock! I'm almost certain she's pregnant,
and if you've been kicking up a fuss about it, you're going to
have to stop it at once." The doctor was now pointing his
index finger in Charlie's face and making sure every point of
his sentence was clearly understood. "You're both young and
healthy, and four kiddies are not too many. I tell you frankly!

She can't stand whatever it is you have been doing to her. I must say I can't understand..."

"You mean she didn't tell you?" Charlie's voice was so patient and concerned that it astounded the Doctor and abruptly cut his lecture short.

"Tell me what? She barely spoke three words the whole time I was examining her."

"Well, her brother...you know Forrey...she just got the wire, not even an hour ago...he was killed in Korea. Killed in some sort of battle."

"Killed?!" The doctor was no longer using his desk for a perch to lecture from, but for a crutch to keep from falling to the floor.

"Yeah, that's what the telegram said. George Potter called just before I got home. You just wait till I get my hands on him! Surely he could have waited the few minutes more it took me to get home with her when she got the news. I got a word or two to say to that George Potter."

"Well, no wonder. No wonder. Yes, I knew Forrey well. In fact, he and Avelle have always been sort of my favorites you might say." The doctor caught himself drifting a bit and breathed in a deep sigh. "Well, my boy, I apologize. I certainly apologize. Should have known it was something like that. You take real good care of that young lady now. She'll have a hard time coming out of this, and if she is pregnant, she could lose the baby. Call me if you need anything, and bring her in next week. I'll be able to tell you for sure about the pregnancy."

Charlie returned to Avelle to get ready to leave. The doctor disappeared into the examining room and returned to

Avelle and Charlie who were leaving the waiting room.

"Here, young lady, you take this in half a glass of water if you don't drop right off to sleep tonight. And no nonsense! No climbing on ladders or repainting the house for a few days. Can't be too careful right now, you know." Seeing that he was unable to tease her into smiling, the doctor sent them on their way and turned his attention to an overweight teenager who had his face in a comic book. The boy was loudly popping bubble gum and swinging his immense leg over the arm of the waiting room chair.

"Well, Daddy, ready for another one?" Avelle spoke thinking she was cheerful. Charlie played along.

"Ready or not, here we go?" he answered whimsically.

"If we don't watch it, we'll be another 'Cheaper by the Dozen.' I don't think I'm quite up for that many."

"Well, Princess, you may have grown up with the O'Brien version, but that is not us." They both loved children, especially their own and felt every one a miracle. However, four children was one thing, twelve was completely different.

They were both quiet as they climbed into Frank's car. Avelle's mind retreated to their wedding and first year of marriage, as if no telegram had ever come of Forrey's death.

When Charlie and Avelle married, Charlie still had another year before his enlistment was up. Their honeymoon was spent getting settled into an apartment near his base. Charlie knew how hard the lonely months would be for Avelle. So before they left, he asked his mother to write to Avelle often to occupy her time.

His mother happily obliged and sent some family

portraits to help her feel more at home. Gladys wanted Avelle to be more connected to their family when they came back home after Charlie's discharge from the Navy. One of the pictures was a really old sepia-toned daguerreotype of Charlie's Great-Grandmother Trappen. She was wearing some huge, barbaric-looking, cross-type ornament that was set with a great stone. Trying to trace Charlie's features in the noble old face, Avelle began to puzzle over the decoration, and finally asked Charlie about it. Seemingly, he had never noticed the jewel before and had no idea what it was or if there was any significance to its existence. To entertain his bride a little, Charlie repeated a family legend of some sort of Norwegian Noble that had descended from the Vikings and had sailed to Northern Ireland, losing his heart to some sweet Colleen, never returning to his homeland.

After absorbing herself thoroughly in this romantic tale, Avelle confided to Charlie that she believed the stone and design of the cross was similar to the jewelry worn only by the Swedish Royal Family, and that if he cared to look into it, he would find that he had royal blood in his veins. If he wanted her to, she would write to the American Consul at Stockholm in Charlie's behalf and find out more about his ancestry. After Charlie finished laughing at her romantic fairy-tale fancies, he wiped the tears his laughter caused. He reminded her that if he could lay claim to descended royalty then so could she, by the marriage-rite. At that moment, Avelle was crowned with the title 'Princess.' It began as a way to poke fun at her, but by now it had become a cherished lover's name.

# CHAPTER 9

"WELL, PRINCESS," CHARLIE SPOKE tenderly as he then shifted gears, "where do you want to go first?"

Charlie's question startled Avelle out of her daydream. "Oh, um. More than likely the City Club?" Clarence was still working at the City Club, if you called what he did work. After he was fired, Clarence had made an effort to look for various work. He had been a harm hand, a ranch hand, a janitor at various businesses, and even worked at the post office for a short time. Clarence pulled himself together with each job and promised not to drink so much, but each job ended the same way. Clarence would either be drunk or hung over and then fired. His only regular, faithful habit was ending up at the City Club, where he would sweep the floors to pay for his tab. There were still a few people in town that had some sympathy for Clarence, and John Smith, owner of City Club, was one of them. He gave Clarence a job working behind the counter and closing up the bar at night. Sometimes there was enough of his paycheck left over after paying his tab, and that made him feel like he was still being a good father and husband.

Charlie turned off Main, crossed the highway that ran through Glenns Ferry, then turned on to Front and pulled up to the 100-year-old-shack-looking bar. Its siding resembled petrified wood. Only one sign hung beside the front door, and it needed to be repainted. Although the sidewalk was always swept clean, the whole building was in desperate need of a wash.

Avelle felt the pulse of her heart rate rise with apprehension as she and Charlie prepared to walk in. Clarence was seated at the bar, head down upon his crossed arms on the counter.

"Drunk as usual," Avelle muttered in disgust.

The attentive looks of the bartender and a seemingly familiar man, who stood with one hand on Clarence's shoulder, alerted them that something besides drink ailed the man who was slumped on his well-reserved stool.

"Oh, Papa, Papa!" Avelle cried as she hurried to her father. The sound of her voice straightened Clarence's back. She could see his face was ravaged by grief.

Clarence opened his arms to Avelle and openly sobbed on her shoulder. "Oh, Baby, Baby! How could we have lived to see this day! Why, oh, why couldn't have God taken me instead, a man of no use to this world? Oh, I'm so sick of living! Why did it have to be him, the finest son a man would ever have? He's everything I always meant to be and never was. Oh, that I should live to see this day!"

The bartender wrinkled his brow with concern and hastily poured a shot of his finest for Clarence, Charlie, and Avelle. Charlie barely stopped the bartender with a motion of his hand and with eyes that proved he was serious.

"Nothing for us. Thanks just the same." The bartender looked at the two presumably recent customers and assumed them to be sanctimonious churchgoers. Nothing could have been farther from the truth.

Charlie had lost his taste for any type of liquor during his service in the Navy, when most men were just beginning their drinking habit. Avelle saw how the drink slowly wrapped around her father like a python capturing its prey. To her, religion (no matter which one a person chose) had nothing to do with drinking. She observed that the merriment or ease of sorrow proved to be short lived. Avelle saw with her own eyes that once the grip had made its hold, its ticking clock of death began. It was the death of trust, death of responsibility, death of true friendship, death to any kind of happy and loving relationship. She felt robbed of her father, and it had obligated Forrey to take on more responsibility. The grip on the father had prevented her brother from living his own life and dreams. Avelle feared that the last one to realize the cost to his life and family, if in fact he could, was the one who had turned again to the bar and had his grip on another glass.

Clarence barely stepped out of his sorrow, to perform the

expected ceremony of introduction. With his head still down only his right hand assisted the introduction.

"You kids know George Potter, I reckon. George, my daughter, Avelle, and her husband, Charlie Brehan. George here just brought me that devil-accursed telegram."

"Just got away a minute ago. Thought I'd bring Clarence the word personally." George Potter confidently explained his presence.

"Oh, you did, did you?" Charlie asked savagely, circling around Avelle to the opposite side of the bar, causing George to reluctantly take his hand off Clarence's shoulder and stand face to face with Charlie.

"Well, I've been hoping to run into you. Why in the name of all that's Holy didn't you hold that phone call until I got home? Haven't you got an ounce of human kindness? She thought the sun rose and set in her brother. Why, there's no telling what she might have done when she heard like that, and me not home with her! Surely it wouldn't have been against the rules to wait a few more minutes until I got home!"

"It was already almost a couple hours since the cable came in as it was," George tried to defend his actions regarding the telegram. "I couldn't find out if you were on the day shift or workin' overtime without letting everyone in on the news. I finally figured that you'd be home in a little while if you were on days. Besides, you know it would be my job if the office knew I'd held that message up two hours."

Charlie's frustration with the timing began to lessen at George's explanation. "Well, I hope I never come that close to punchin' a guy for doing me a favor." Though still not completely satisfied, Charlie returned to Avelle after a gentleman's handshake of truce.

A big brassy blonde in a lovely blue lace dress was sitting on a stool nearest the door and had eyed Charlie when the couple had first walked in the bar. She had been attracted to Charlie and had hoped that his obvious air of ill-ease had meant that there was discontentment with his companion and a possible opening for her. While ordering another drink, she made some inquiries of the bartender. After acquainting herself with the facts, she moved to a stool close to Avelle and offered her a sack of nuts to share, as if to atone for her previous intentions.

Munching on the nuts had made Avelle ravenously hungry, so when Charlie rejoined her, she asked to be taken to dinner. They had asked Clarence to join them, but he told them he had already eaten at four o'clock and wasn't hungry, and to go on ahead and not to mind about him.

"You sure you're going to be all right, Papa?"

"Why, Honey, I reckon I ain't never again gonna be 'all right!' I ain't been for some time now, and a thing like this is enough to put a good man under." Clarence heaved his breath with every sentence. "But I'm as right as I'm gonna get to be, and I won't have you worryin' that pretty head over a hulk like me. Your old Papa is a gone goose. The best days were when you were little. Not a cloud in the sky. But the clouds came, you see. The clouds came. I thought I could hold them off, but I wasn't as strong as I made out to be. Most ain't, I'm afraid. When you think of me, remember it takes a pretty good man to keep the sky swept clear. I reckon there's a little good in me or I'd never of fathered a boy like Forrey."

He turned to look his daughter in the eyes. "Don't you forget that, Baby! Seems I remember you better when you were around three or four and you were a real little doll. And here you have kids of your own. It don't seem real. Oh, well." Clarence turned back to his drink with the resignation of giving up life and hope.

Avelle stepped closer and confided to him that she was undoubtedly expecting another child. She had hoped that the joyous news would break his cloud for a moment. But instead, he lifted his shot halfway up off the counter and cheered. "Well, if that don't beat all! I guess we are replaceable." Then he threw the shot down his throat in an unsuccessful attempt to quiet his nerves and sorrow. Avelle determined to never stop trying to break his dark clouds, though she despised the perch her father refused to get down from and the behavior that went with it.

Knowing how hungry Avelle was, Charlie took Avelle by the hand and led her out to the car. Clarence would be on his perch till closing, and now Frank would soon be hunting them up himself.

Frank was just crossing the street when Charlie and Avelle came out of the bar. "I was hoping I would find you both here. Ready to go eat?"

"Why, Frank! You look real handsome."

"Why, thank you Ma'am. Here let me open the door for you." Frank opened the passenger door for Avelle and bowed.

"Boy, get a little hair cut and he turns into a regular Richard Burton!" Charlie gruffly teased.

"Shh. Don't tell Maud." Frank gave a whimsical wink to Charlie, who in turn tossed Frank his keys.

The small group re-parked on the next block in front of the newly reconstructed restaurant. Barry Poindexter replaced the outside siding and tan-colored stucco with a rust-orange border that wrapped around the top of the building, trying to portray a typical adobe-Spanish-type structure. When they walked in, they found that the dinner rush had only filled up less than half the brown wicker tables and booths. Charlie found a booth in the corner hoping for privacy, which was quite easy seeing the lack of patrons.

"Barry better get back on good relations with the Rails or this place won't survive," Avelle stated sympathetically and slipped to the inside of the booth.

"And everyone else in town, by the looks of it." Charlie added.

Frank slid into his seat opposite the couple when Charlie began remarking about the decor.

"Sure makes you think of Mexico. What do you suppose that thing is over there?" Charlie pointed to a décor piece on the opposite wall.

"I think that's meant to be an Aztec shield. I think it's a phony, though. But the other stuff is authentic enough." Frank answered.

"How do you know that?" Avelle was puzzled Frank knew so much about Barry's décor.

"Robert Bahr told me when I was at the barbers. He said Barry took a vacation down to Mexico last year and bought everything you see on the walls."

Barry Poindexter had taken his family down to Mexico for Spring Break the year before, and had thought he had stumbled upon a perfect idea to expand his bar. He decided to remodel with an ancient Mexican motif and slowly introduce Mexican entrees. Barry dreamed about his place becoming a restaurant of culture, whose fame would spread like wildfire among the travelers. With all the excitement of an untamed entrepreneurial spirit, he saw his new restaurant as putting Glenns Ferry on the map as a destination stop, not just a resting place on the road to somewhere else.

Barry turned the bar into a dining area for the restaurant and expanded the back to include a private bar where food could also be served. The restaurant and bar were painted with chocolate brown walls and colorful yellow, red, and blue frieze that wrapped unbroken along the top of the walls. Each booth along the two sides had different sombreros, stings of red and green ceramic chili peppers, and Aztec worship masks with decorative saddle blankets as a backdrop, along with the decorative shield that Charlie had noticed.

To keep with somewhat of an authentic theme, Barry had imported his help that indubitably violated the code of the Railroad towns of Glenns Ferry and King Hill. The code, 'We take care of our own,' is never more understood than during the lay-off season. The Railroad workers are not tied to the same seasons as farmers or ranchers. Their seasons are tied to contracts that the Company Representative is able to secure with clients and customers. The unspoken code is that during 'lay-offs', the bars, restaurants, stores, ranches, farms, etc. give the out-of-work Railroaders the first crack at employment. Barry's quest for something original in the small town of Glenns Ferry put him on difficult terms with the majority of the townsfolk.

One of the bartenders came through the swinging doors from the back, sat down coffee and water in front of Charlie and Avelle, and sat down a beer in front of Frank. Charlie looked inquisitively at the bartender and noticed him exchanging an understood look with Frank.

"What?" Frank asked looking back at Charlie. "I didn't know what you wanted."

Charlie just shook his head knowing there was nothing to do but enjoy his coffee.

"Do you folks wish to order?" The bartender asked. There was no accent to assume Barry had not hired a local. He was slight Basque. Then again there was about as many Basque as there was Irish, and they all considered themselves Idahoans.

"Yes, thank you," answered Charlie.

On his way back to the bar the bartender bellowed, 'Customers!' into the kitchen. A waitress came immediately from the kitchen and handed them their menus. All three looked at the menus with a little surprise. None of the selection seemed to resemble anything like Mexican food. Waiting in her orange short-sleeved dress uniform with a blue bib apron, she held her pencil to her notepad, seemingly patiently waiting.

Frank had barely looked at the menu when he ordered. "Tommy got my mouth to watering talking about prawns. Bring me prawns, Ma'am!"

"Rib steak for me, medium. Princess?"

"Rib steak for me, too. Very well done, thank you." Avelle smiled. And the waitress left to go fill their order. "I thought Barry was supposed to be serving Mexican food?"

"Had your heart set on a Mexican dinner, eh, Princess?"

"I did, but that's okay. I'm so hungry I could care less what I eat."

Charlie had never seen his wife so calm, so detached. There was shrillness to her voice. He knew the inevitable break-up was just under her false reserve. After the trio finished their dinner, Charlie asked for the check only to find that Frank had paid for the dinner before he initially sat down.

They emerged from the restaurant as the dusk was surrendering to the dark starlit night, and the small town was coming alive with the warm summer evening. The neon lights of businesses that were still open and the street lights along Main Street begged to assist the glow of the heavenly stars and the bold, bright moon.

"Charlie! Frank! Look! Look!" Peaking above the buildings, a Ferris wheel with its bright flashing lights had caught Avelle's attention. "A carnival must have just come to town. Let's go over and have some fun."

"Sure you don't want to just go home, Princess?" Charlie dreaded being out amongst the crowd, not knowing how much of the town had now found out about Forrey's death.

"Oh, you're no fun. And no, I don't want to go home! If you don't want to be my escort, then sit in the car and Frank and I will go!"

"Oh, hey, now, keep me out of this one." Frank put his hands up in a sign of surrender.

"Oh, calm down. I was just asking, Princess. I think a carnival sounds like a great idea. Besides, with Frank paying for dinner I have yet to spend a penny since we've been in town." Charlie had no intention of being the one who broke Avelle's reserve.

To Charlie's relief, as the threesome walked about the carnival at the fair grounds, no one mentioned Forrey. To the friends and acquaintances they met in their stroll, it only appeared as though Charlie and Avelle were (at best) annoyed with each other. During the festivities, Charlie had stopped to play a ring-toss game, and easily pitched the yellow rubber rings over three of the bottles and won a poor excuse for a teddy bear. It was as big as their youngest daughter, Nancy Ann, with a red felt vest and brown fur that kept shedding onto Charlie's clothes and sticking to his hands. Avelle refused to take it home to the kids and Charlie was quite the sight, trying to give it away to anyone they met. Finally, as they turned toward the Ferris wheel, Charlie chucked the bear behind a clump of sagebrushes.

From year to year, Frank always enjoyed the carnival but never once went on a ride. "I like my feet firmly planted on the ground," he would always say whenever Maud wanted to ride. Tonight was no different. So Charlie and Avelle went ahead and took their seats, but after a couple revolutions, Avelle's stomach started to turn faster than the Ferris wheel and begged to be let off. Charlie could not have felt more grateful that Avelle finally wanted to go home.

# CHAPTER 10

AS THEY PILED BACK in the car, Avelle noticed the cornucopia of roses wrapped in the newspaper. "Oh, no! Maud's roses! They're all wilted! I was supposed to take them to Mrs. Henderson after my visit. Now what am I going to do?"

"We'll just have to get some more." Frank could see the tears forming in Avelle's eyes and was determined to not let Avelle's promise go undone.

"Oh yeah? Where? Are we going to dash to the Florist in Boise tonight?" Charlie was curious of Frank's intention.

"There's plenty of flowers around town here. They're just in their prime. Why, I seen the prettiest bushes of Paul's-Scarlet on old Gus's garage I ever seen in my life."

Charlie wondered if the beers Frank had at dinner were

now affecting his judgment. "Right! And you're just going to go over to old Gus and ask him for some of his flowers?"

Old Gus wasn't very well liked. He was a Conductor for the Railroad and fought bitterly against the compulsory retirement. He had ignored the optimal retirement age of sixty-five. Then he spent his last five years, before the inevitable mandatory retirement, constantly talking about what he would say to the Company if they presumed to tell him he was unfit for further service. It was a severe blow to his pride when they unceremoniously retired him, paying not one iota of heed to his protests. Nevertheless, he still came over to the depot in Glens Ferry to keep a sharp watch on everything as if he was made an honorary Official. After making himself a sufficient nuisance, he was officially banned from any Company property.

After that, he hung around the bars for awhile, but a long-standing ulcer made a poor customer, and with his 'jolly' attitude was banished from all the bars too. Finally, he turned to the garden around his spacious home. Old Gus grew more bitter than the year before, carrying a continual grievance for the Company and resented every working man.

Frank drove his DeSoto in the direction of old Gus's so the couple would have the best view of the magnificent display of blooms. Nearing the place, they saw Gus walking toward town. The house was dark, so they assumed Gus's wife must be asleep. The stars that had earlier lit the sky now had lost some of their brightness, or at least around old Gus's house.

"Let's get out of the car and have a closer look." Both Charlie and Avelle looked at Frank like he was as crazy as old Gus was bitter; however, the school-boy excitement in Frank's eyes gave way to their reservations, and they tip-toed across the lawn for a closer view.

Old Gus had secured a lattice wall where the massive rosebush grew in a magnificent perfection against one side of the garage. They stood before it with breathless awe as their eyes jumped from cluster to cluster.

Charlie whispered in wonder and reverence. "Old Gus can sure grow roses." Frank and Avelle could only agree with a nod of their heads.

As the eyes of the trespassers looked over the bounty of the well-tended Paul's-Scarlet, they saw a double border of bushes. Roses in every conceivable color formed a hedge around the perfect lawn, situated a foot or so from the sidewalk so passers by couldn't pick them. The house stood center on a corner lot, with the garage next to the alley. The roses extended from the Paul's-Scarlet then turned from the alleyway around the corner, along the side of the property and around to border the sidewalk in front. The house was a squat brick with siding structure. Out the myriad of windows old Gus kept a vigilant watch for anyone bold enough to stop and admire his work. Old Gus had planted a thick line of lilac bushes in the inside line of his lot to prevent his neighbor from ever enjoying the paradise he had created. If old Gus had thought it possible to border his whole property with the lilacs, he most certainly would have done it.

Charlie walked over to the border and glanced up and down the darkened street. After turning around and looking back at the house, he said, "You know, I've got half a notion to..."

Frank broke off Charlie's sentence with, "Yeah!" And with the same idea in both their minds, drew their pocketknives like little boys with their play swords.

They began removing roses savagely and indiscriminately. While they were piling them in Avelle's arms, Avelle glanced at the house with a little bit of guilt.

"Don't take too much, Honey. Think how his wife would feel!"

"His wife!" Charlie halfway yelled. His eyes glanced up at the house almost fearful that he had awakened Gus's wife. He spoke again more softly but still scornfully, "do you think old Gus ever lets her cut any of them?"

"Well, it's not right to take so many of them without leaving something in return," Avelle protested. "Oh, I know!" An idea then struck her mind. Avelle sat the roses on the ground, dashed to the car, picked up Maud's wilted roses, and began to arrange them about the base of the rose bush as a peace offering. She then took the now empty newspaper and wrapped up the newly cut roses into her arms. The trio looked cautiously around and scampered back to the car, knowing that if old Gus caught them, he would insist on them being arrested.

It was with a definite sense of relief that they reached the car undetected. Once safely away, the thrill and hilarity knew no bounds. They began looking into the flowerbeds on either side of the street with trespassing malice. No longer silent, they raided several other flowerbeds, and laughed triumphantly at each new successful bundle. To make amends for their sinful night, they did their best not to strip mercilessly and had decided to leave the meager displays strictly alone. Near the end of their flower raid, they spied a tin oval washtub that was the perfect size for a vase, so they took that, too. Frank pulled up to the side of Doc's home, and Charlie let Avelle into the backseat to put together the flower arrangement.

"I doubt Mrs. Henderson will ever get another bouquet like this one." Avelle smiled proudly after putting the finishing touches on the arrangement.

"No, I don't expect so." Charlie agreed.

"Here, wait a minute!" Frank took out his pen and began hastily looking for something on which to write. Mindlessly he pulled out his checkbook and wrote rapidly on the back of the check. This idea almost sent the young couple into hysterical laughter after seeing the note. It read: "*To Mrs. Henderson with oceans of love. An unknown Admirer.*"

Although Mrs. Henderson was considered a very nice lady, she was easily the ugliest woman any of them had ever seen and was considered a horrible comparison to every woman in town. There must have been a Mr. Henderson at some point, or somewhere, but for as long as any of them could remember; she was the Doctor's housekeeper. They had seen a light on in the housekeeper's quarters, and to complete their adolescent night of trespassing and thievery they rang the bell and fled to the car.

When they reached home, their state of exhilaration and the late hour shocked Maud half out of her senses. Maud had taken the children over to the Brehan's and put them to bed several hours ago. After Avelle apologized for being so late, she thanked Maud for watching the children. Maud walked home by herself. Maud was about to lecture Frank when she found him passed out on their bed with his clothes still on.

At the Brehan home, Charlie and Avelle were half asleep themselves when the clatter and roar of an approaching freight train drove thoughts of sleep away. At the height of the noise, Charlie laughed and said something that Avelle didn't catch. She rolled over and screamed, 'What?' in his ear, and he laughingly repeated his words. Most of it was still lost in the clatter, but she understood his mirth, for one phrase became clear, 'an unknown admirer!' She went off into a gale of laughter and they both lost all interest in Mrs. Henderson, the train, and their fatigue.

`Charlie and Avelle met at a Fourth of July dance almost ten years prior, when Charlie was on leave. He was the first sailor she had ever seen. He was almost too handsome to be believed in his regulation whites, with his cap tucked under his arm, showing off his thick, wavy, red hair. Avelle had never before believed in love at first sight until Charlie. His manner was all but regal as he surveyed the local girls whirling about the floor. Although Avelle had gone to the dance with his brother, Louie, the two had never met before that night. Once introduced, they danced together the rest of the evening. By some arrangement, Charlie ended up taking her home in Louie's car. He hardly spoke as he took her home, and Avelle feared Charlie thought her too immature. When they reached her home, she was surprised at the urgency he had in asking for a date.

They were together constantly for the rest of his leave. The O'Brien brood immediately took him into their collective hearts, and Avelle was surprised that the Brehan family were so all-American. Louie was the only Brehan Avelle really knew and she had never before been on their ranch or in their home. When it was time for Charlie to leave, Forrey took them both to the train. His leaving shattered her, and her first two letters were tear-stained. Charlie was love sick, too. Before receiving his first letter, he called her from base and asked if she had any objection to bearing the Brehan name for the rest of her life.

They had a fairy-tale wedding in the fall, a year and a half later. Avelle's simple dress was made with her mother's wedding lace, and Charlie was in his regulation whites that he wore when they met. Everything was so special and so right, everybody on their very best behavior. Not a cloud marred the sky. Friends and relatives, flashbulbs and wedding cake, tears and laughter filled the autumn sky. Avelle would never again in her life see a man in a military uniform without some romantic memory of that perfect day.

# CHAPTER 11

THE ALARM THAT SET upon Avelle's vanity dresser blasted its bell to wake the sleeping adults. Avelle reluctantly rose from her bed to prepare Charlie's breakfast and found their clothes still laying where they had tossed them indiscriminately the night before. After getting dressed, she entered the kitchen and could tell that Maud had tried to clean up. Avelle was grateful for Maud's help but also embarrassed about leaving such a mess before they had left for town. The bathtub had been wiped out and the towels along with Charlie's work clothes were draped over the side. The sun was trying to help, too. It peaked above the horizon beckoning the day to be bright and cheerful, but its effort would not be successful for this little home.

In preparing breakfast, she burnt the eggs. While the

coffee was percolating on the stove, she clumsily knocked it to the floor spilling its entire contents. In cleaning the pan and floor she let Charlie oversleep. Hustling to remake both the eggs and coffee, she burnt the eggs again. Charlie was trying to be helpful, which somehow made the morning that much worse. She ordered him out of the house with barely a few sips of coffee. When Avelle went to take the coffee off the stove for her morning cup, she ended up burning her hand on the handle. With her right hand wrapped up with ointment for the burn, she sunk into her chair at the table to attempt a few peaceful sips.

As the sun began to rise up over the horizon, it pleaded with Avelle to step outside and be refreshed in its glow and warmth. Avelle could see Maud's beautiful new white chenille top sheet blowing gently on the line. Her eyes turned to see the section crew unloading ice from the boxcar that was apparently left during the night. Few things soothed Avelle's heart more than to see men working. She treasured and appreciated Charlie's help around the house, but she loved it more to see him and other men working. It spoke of the man; was he faithful, dependable, and useful? Did he complain, make excuses, or finish the job? Could you see his pride, his effort, or his talent? Avelle reasoned to herself that the same evaluation made for those who worked to bring home a paycheck could also be made for those who stayed home to take care of the family.

Avelle had stepped off the front stoop and come around the house to watch the men. She was old enough to remember well her father's blundering catastrophe, but couldn't help but watch the whole process with wonder and excitement. The crisp morning air and the lustrous sun smiled upon the men as they guided the great blocks of ice down the plank runway and into the lonely chilled and dark icehouse. To one side of the icehouse lay a pile of back straw soup that the men had extracted. To the opposite side lay a new golden pile of sawdust that was to be shoveled over the new ice. The aroma of the sawdust danced upon the air with a pine-fresh scent that drew Avelle unknowingly to the fence that separated Railroad Row and the working area and tracks.

Charlie had glanced up from his tally-sheet on his metal clipboard and saw Avelle standing at the fence. He thought that she wanted some ice and spoke to the Foreman. Fred Davis was a dry-wry-humored bachelor that the Company had transferred from Pocatello to replace her father. Davis was 6'3" with broad shoulders and weighed barely 180 pounds, and not much younger than her father. He was known for following Company rules and regulations to the very letter. So when Davis offered Charlie the Foreman's Section house and began rooming at the Brunnell's home, the surprise and gratefulness of the Brehan's knew no bounds.

Davis was shouting to Avelle as he crossed the tracks. Avelle shook her head and pointed to her ear saying she didn't understand him.

"Oh. Sorry, Mrs. Brehan. I was asking if you wanted some ice."

"Oh, no. I was just watching you men work. I've never

really watched the ice being unloaded before."

"Would you like to have a better view?"

"Really?!" Avelle was surprised at this unexpected honor, and she seemed almost to skip as she walked up the path across the tracks to Charlie's side.

Charlie was all business with his count and only gave his wife a brief welcoming smile without saying a word. Hammett had sent a section crew up to help with the unloading so that plenty of men were stationed at every step, efficiently guiding the process. It was as if each time ice was transferred, the men determined to never again repeat that tragic accident of seventeen years ago. Avelle watched as men in the ice-car maneuvered each block to the doorway of the freight car and onto the plank runway with care. Each block was guided easily and watchfully into the icehouse to rest upon the sawdust in patchwork style until extracted for use, or it melted to create the year-end's slop.

"Amazing, isn't it?" Avelle whipped her head to Charlie, but her eyes betrayed her ears. She had heard Forrey's voice. Tears stung in her eyes. Avelle could feel Forrey's presence, and it was as if she had awakened to the reality that he wasn't there. She turned without a word and dashed back to the house. Charlie, watching his wife flee, contemplated whether he should ask for the rest of the day off.

Taking a step closer to Charlie, Davis spoke in a low private voice, saying, "I see no reason why you can't take off after lunch, if you feel you need to."

With Charlie's eyes fixed for the moment on his home, he answered, "I appreciate that, Davis, thank you. I sure am glad our work orders kept us close by home today." With Charlie's eyes back on the tally-sheet, he committed to focus his attention on the work at hand, but the care for his wife's sorrow betrayed his own grief.

Avelle wiped the tears from her eyes as the sun was fully shining its rays into her home betraying hidden cobwebs in their various corners. Everywhere she looked, she saw a dirty and disorderly house. The sleepy-eyed children were waking up and calling out for breakfast, which forced Avelle's grief again into second place. First she had to get the children fed and dressed and then get the house cleaned before someone saw her home in such an untidy state. She scoured, scrubbed, dusted, mopped, and picked up. Although satisfied that the house was ready to greet anyone who might venture to call, she would rather prefer it if the world would just stay away.

# CHAPTER 12

WITH THE TRANSFER OF the icehouse complete, the Hammett crew left to go back to their section. Charlie saw that Avelle had been keeping herself busy and talked to Davis about working on some minor repairs at the yard. He wanted to keep an eye on her without getting in her way.

Mama, what are we having for lunch?" asked Kath with a slight whine. Avelle could hardly believe her oldest daughter would be going to school in just a few short months.

"How about tuna sandwiches?"

"Can we have soda, too?" Kath's slight whine turned into a hopeful plea.

"Do you think you can go to Brunnell's store and bring some home?"

"Oh, yes, Mama. And I promise to be extra careful

crossing the highway."

Avelle walked Kath to the highway and watched her cross. Only after Kath was safe in the store did Avelle return back into the house. While Kath was at the store, Avelle made the tuna sandwiches and opened her last jar of pickles that Maud had canned with her prize pickle recipe. Nancy Ann was satisfied with the tuna mixture, and Chuckie was content with a pickle while waiting for the 'special treat.'

As Avelle looked at her two younger children, a tear fell from her eyes. She began to again feel the sting of her heart tearing within her soul. She might have at that moment allowed herself to finally surrender to her pain, but just then she heard a car turn off the highway, pulling up to her home. Somehow she would have to be strong. Somehow she would have to be brave. Her grief was now just a breath away from breaking through the dam she had less than twenty-four hours ago.

A lovely blonde in a lilac tie-silk dress had stepped and walked up to the gate. She parked her purple 1947 Ford Sportsman with wood trimmed doors that wrapped around to the trunk next to the Brehan's Jalopy. Avelle took a quick glance at the store and saw Maud coming out with Kath. Avelle left the front door and came toward the stranger, thinking to herself, "Another tourist wanting directions, I suppose."

"Are you Mrs. Brehan? Mrs. Charles Brehan?"

"Yes. May I help you?" Avelle was taken a back by a stranger who apparently knew her name.

"May I speak with you for a moment?" The stranger

seemed to have been clutching something in her hands, something that resembled mail, peaking Avelle's curiosity.

"Certainly. Won't you come in?" Avelle couldn't have been more relieved that she had taken the morning to clean her home and could unashamedly welcome any guest who approached her door.

"Thank you, but no. I can't stay." The young lady looked down at her possession with apprehension, trying to find the courage to speak. Avelle couldn't help but notice how the stranger's hat and shoes matched her dress perfectly. Her blonde hair fell just over an inch below her shoulders with perfect curls at the ends. She was the same height as Avelle, and it looked as though they might very well be the same size.

"I feel like I have an unfair advantage," the young lady continued. "I feel like I know you so well, and of course, you don't know who I am." The young lady took one hand off her possession and offered it to Avelle introducing herself. "My name is Gloria, Gloria O'Neal. I work at Hammacks, in the office."

Grateful for the introduction, Avelle took her hand and looked Miss O'Neal in the eyes. It was as if she was looking at her twin, only with blonde hair. "It's a pleasure to meet you. Wait, I think I do know you. Didn't you come out and tell the saleslady about the sizes in that metallic green dress I was looking at the after Christmas sales?"

"Oh, of course. Now I remember. How could I have forgotten that? Size eight, right? I told Forrest I'd never seen you before." Gloria's eyes sparkled at the memory.

"Forrey?" Avelle began to lose the strength of her legs.

Miss O'Neal came through the gate, to offer her assistance. "Here, let's sit here on the step." Miss O'Neal continued after they had sat down. "I guess Forrest didn't tell you he had met me."

Avelle shook her head, more in an effort to regain a clear thought than answering the lady who was sitting next to her. Avelle noticed the package that rested on Miss O'Neal's lap were letters and obviously written in Forrey's handwriting. They were secured on all four sides with a deep red silk ribbon tied in a bow that covered the address.

Avelle tried to speak, but the polite questions that were straining to form in her mind were paralyzed in her throat. Miss O'Neal took out a handkerchief from her purse and offered it to Avelle, who received it obligingly. Miss O'Neal began to share the story that she had been rehearsing all night.

"I was staying with my sister in San Antonio, while my former boyfriend and his band were booking gigs in Galveston. They booked a benefit dance at Sheppard Air Force Base and, as always, I went along for the ride." Miss O'Neal stopped and stared daydreaming towards the highway and confessed, "You know, I went down to Texas thinking how romantic the showbiz life would be, but frankly I was beginning to get a little tired of the whole bunch. The more I went on the tour, the more the romance fizzled." Miss O'Neal turned and smiled at Avelle and Avelle saw a little sorrow in this stranger's eyes.

Across the highway, Maud was walking with Kath. Avelle

could tell they must have walked somewhere else because now they were again reaching the store. She could have sworn she had just seen them come out a minute ago.

"So at the benefit dance on the base," continued Miss O'Neal, "I went wandering around and ran into Forrest. Apparently, he had just been assigned Mechanic First and didn't have a soul with whom he could share his news. He seemed so lonely too, and then he began talking about you and showing me your picture." Avelle smiled with a little shake of her head in embarrassment but didn't interrupt her guest's story. "At first I thought it was the same old line, you know, 'Say you remind me of my sister,' but Forrest wasn't like that at all. He was sweet, and he sure loved you."

"What brought you all the way up here from Texas?" Avelle couldn't help but ask.

"My grandmother fell last fall and broke her leg just below the knee. I moved in to help her out until she improved. Do you know her, Elvira Potts? She lives in town." Miss O'Neal looked at Avelle, who dabbed her eyes again with the handkerchief and shook her head to say, 'no.'

Miss O'Neal rose up and turned to face Avelle. "I feel like these belong to you, more than they belong to me." Miss O'Neal handed the inch and a half thick stack of letters tied with their ribbon to Avelle, who stood up to receive them. "After Forrest shipped out, he wrote to me now and then. I thought you should have them since they're mainly about you and your kids and Charlie."

Avelle walked Miss O'Neal to her car, as Maud was helping Kath across the highway. Avelle found her voice enough to thank the young messenger. Just before Miss O'Neal slipped behind the wheel, she spoke as if a dream had just danced away with the wind.

"What a nice guy. I just knew you'd be just as nice. It was really wonderful to meet you."

"Who was that?" Maud asked curiously.

"Gloria O'Neal. Forrey was writing her." Avelle's words were uttered with barely any breath. She turned toward the house and walked as though drifting in a fog, while staring at the letters she was just given. Falling into the first chair the senses of her body could find, she pulled at the end of one of the ribbons. Her hands began to tremble as she reopened the first letter. She felt like she was intruding upon the privacy of her brother, but couldn't help being curious about his savoir-faire in dealing with the fairer sex.

Avelle knew his character and courage strengthened with each responsibility required by the war, but each reopened letter betrayed his loneliness.

"Oh, why didn't I write him more?! Why couldn't I have told him how proud I was of him?! Why wasn't I praying for him?!"

The last reprimand that escaped from her tear-filled mouth became the dagger that pierced her heart. Avelle leapt from her chair and dashed to her bedroom, leaving the scattered letters and tossed ribbon to lay exposed on the hardwood floor. The bedroom door slammed shut, and the beloved sister wept bitterly upon her bed as if to seal herself into the same coffin that now held her brother.

The grace of God was closer to Avelle than she realized.

Tears were never given as a means of manipulation, nor to show a childish mind. They are the rain that heals a mountainside that has been ravaged by fire. They are the sap that heals the wounded tree. They are heaven-sent to wash away the bitter residue when a heart breaks. Though the wrong may never be made right and the farewell never properly spoken, the unbearable pain must somehow be borne.

Charlie had entered the home just as the bedroom door rested, concealing the bitter sorrow. Maud rose from the table where the children were silently eating. Charlie already knew the answer to his first question, but he asked Maud anyway.

"Where's Avelle?"

"Oh, Charlie! It's just awful, isn't it! Avelle just now ran into her room."

"Where did all these letters come from?" Charlie walked back over to the discarded letters and Maud followed to give him what information she could.

"Avelle said that they were from a girl Forrey was writing to, a Gloria O'Neal, I think she said. Did Forrey find a girl? Oh, Charlie, just when he was finally going to start to settle down. It's just so awful." Maud wiped away the tears that were already halfway down her face. "I met Kath in the store, and when we got back across the highway, Avelle was saying goodbye to a very pretty blonde."

"Daddy, we got the mail for you." Kath offered the unopened mail to her father, hoping to cheer him.

"I didn't know if you or Avelle had checked it in the last

few days. I hope you don't mind, I helped Kath get your mail."

"Oh, thanks. Thank you, Kitten." Charlie took the mail and set it on one of the end tables. Then bent down to try to piece together the letters on the floor.

"Well, Charlie why don't you come over to our house for dinner. Or after dinner, I can help you put the children to bed."

"Thank you Maud, we should be fine." Charlie didn't look up at Maud when he answered her. Maud said goodbye to the children and left for her own home sharing the grief of those still inside. Charlie put the letters in one pile, the envelopes in another, and the few letters that were not reopened in yet another pile. He wanted to look at them, but that would have to wait until he had checked on his wife and put his children to bed.

# CHAPTER 13

AFTER CHARLIE HAD STACKED the piles together, he put them on top of the mail he had just set on the end table. As he came toward the kitchen table he looked down the hallway to the shut door, his boots felt like they had cement stuck to them instead of sawdust as he walked to the bedroom door and turned the round, iron knob. Avelle had her back to the door laying in a fetal position with the multi-colored patchwork quilt she made in their first year of marriage. She had never made a quilt before, so her mother-in-law sent Avelle scrapes of fabric and some patterns. The long lonely days when Charlie was still in the Navy were filled by the countless patient hours needed to stitch a quilt worth using. Now the quilt draped over Avelle's sobbing body as she clutched one end to her heart.

"Princess?" Charlie spoke softly.

"Get out of here and just leave me alone!" Charlie's pillow came flying at the door and would have hit his forehead perfectly had he not closed the door.

Slowly, Charlie headed back to the kitchen table where his children sat. He could see that Maud must have made him a sandwich before she left, because Avelle was not expecting him home. Kath had only eaten half of her sandwich and was watching her father's every move. Chuckie had finished his lunch and was now enjoying the last few sips of his soda. Nancy Ann sat in her metal highchair chewing on Maud's pickle as juice washed down her chin and right arm onto the metal tray.

"Daddy, is Mama sad?" Kath asked sympathetically as Charlie sat down to his plate.

"Yes, Peaches she is very sad."

"Is it because Uncle Forrey died?"

The question struck Charlie. They had not told the children, and yet here was his oldest asking a direct and mature question. "Yes, Peaches. Uncle Forrey died."

"How did he die?" Chuckie asked after he finished off his last sip.

"Well, son, we only know right now is that he died while fighting for our country."

"Is Uncle Forrey a hero?" questioned Kath.

"Yes Peaches. He is." Charlie reached out and stroked his daughter's forehead and cheek.

"Did he shoot bad guys?" Chuckie looked at his father.

"Yes, son, he did." Charlie began to pick up his sandwich.

"But if Uncle Forrey was a hero, how come he died? Only the bad guys die." A plain serious face remained on his little boy while waiting for an answer. Charlie struggled for words that could satisfy his son's answer without destroying the faith and belief that the good guy, the hero, always wins the fight. The hero walks away from the fight without blood on his face and his white hat still on his head, while the bad guy is sprawled out face down on the dirt road, dead.

Charlie looked at his son, "That's the way it should be, son, but it doesn't always work out like that." Chuckie looked down at his plate trying to process his father's answer. "Why don't you put your plate in the sink and go play outside?" To Charlie's relief, Chuckie seemed to accept his father's answer and went back outside to play with his truck. Kath sat in her chair with her hands in her lap. Her eyes were staring down on her half eaten lunch, but her mind was forming questions she had never thought before. Kath wanted to talk not play.

Her questions were no longer the innocent: Where is God? Why is the sky blue? Why does it rain? Her questions required deeper answers, they came from a mind trying to understand why her world would not just require the grass to grow but would also ask for men to die. Why is there war? Isn't everybody free? What is freedom?

These moments with children are more tender and crucial than the farmer knowing the moment the soil is ready to receive the seeds for his crop. They plant the magnetic pointer into their compass that they will use to direct their lives. Willingly, Charlie took his time to give his daughter the same honesty in his answers as she had in her questions.

This conversation with her father carved a lasting memory in her soul. Kath would say that she remembered vividly a statement her father had made about freedom. "Peaches, freedom tests what is important to an individual and to the people as a nation. When people live under tyranny or communism they can never express or explore what is in their heart. They cannot think what they wish, live like they want, or believe what they will. We have been given a great gift and the freedom we have shows the world what is in our heart."

The father and daughter's conversation ended with the afternoon almost over and Doc rapping on the screen door.

"Afternoon, Doc. It's like you read my mind, I was just about to call you." The two men shook hands before Doc entered the home.

"Mrs. Hendersen wanted me so tell her secret admirer, 'thank you'. So I thought I would come check on Avelle while I was here in the neighborhood." Doc gave Charlie a wink as Charlie blushed when he remembered that he had completely forgotten about last night. Charlie stepped to the side as the Doc took the lead to the bedroom door.

"Avelle? It's Doc. May I come in?"

Charlie didn't hear Avelle's answer and as the door opened it pushed Charlie's pillow that lay on the floor aside to let Doc in the room. Charlie stayed outside the door while the Doc gave her a sedative. The Doc closed the door behind him, and both men walked back to the front door. Doc gripped Charlie's hand and looked him straight in the eye.

"She's in real bad shape, son. The sedative I just gave her

should help her sleep. You call me, if you need anything."

After dinner with the Warnick's, the Brehan children went straight to bed. When most Fathers put their children to bed it's as if it's just another game they play with their daddy, but not tonight.

"Daddy, you forgot to pray with us." Chuckie's reprimand took Charlie by surprise.

"You're right son, I'm sorry. Which of you would like to pray?" Usually it was Avelle's bedtime ritual to read a story and pray with them, but tonight Charlie would step in.

"Me!" Chuckie spoke up as he pointed his thumbs to his chest.

"Okay, Son, go ahead." Charlie sat at the edge of Kath's bed as they all folded their hands and closed their eyes.

"Dear Jesus, Uncle Forrey is up there with you, so take care of him 'cuz he's a hero. Help Mama not to be so sad. Be wiff Papa, and Auntie Nell, and Nora, and Dora, and Timmy, and Jimmy, and Vince, and Margy, and Connie, and Arlene, Freddie, and Fay, and Teddy, and Jody, Amen."

"Amen" echoed Charlie and Kath. Then Charlie left the room with the door open as the children, feeling the fatigue of their parents sorrow and sad, they themselves drifted off to sleep.

If there had been a way for Charlie to look in on his wife invisibly, he would have done it. But since physics and matter are what they are, Charlie did his best to open their bedroom door as silently as possible. Avelle was still in the same fetal position as he saw her in before. Thankfully, she appeared to be sleeping. Charlie thought how he wanted to lie beside his wife, ease her sorrow, fix her grief, give her all the reasons why it was her brother that died, but he knew better.

When the tragedy of death comes, it matters not how many suffer, because their grief and how they must arise from the ashes of their heart is as personal and individual as their fingerprint. Charlie closed the door and walked to the icebox where there was just enough lemonade for one more glass.

Charlie stood on the porch as the sun shone fully in the west as its rays sang its lullaby across a baby blue sky. He was grateful that his children didn't have to learn about war or fighting for freedom with their own eyes. His family would mourn the loss of their beloved Forrey in the privacy of their home and in the quietness of the night.

Looking over at the old Jalope, Charlie remembered how Forrey answered Charlie's appeal for another year with the 'old-rat-trap.' "You're not gonna get another year out of her. You'd be better off just letting her rust over peacefully in some field." Charlie smiled sadly to himself, tapped the toe of his sawdust covered boot against the porch then scraped the sole of his shoe and walked back inside.

Fatigue began to taunt Charlie as he sat down in his black La-Z-Boy recliner by the window and picked up one of the letters Forrey had written.

*Dear Gloria,*

*I hope this letter finds you and your sisters' family healthy and happy.*

*We have finally arrived here in Korea. I thought the base in Texas was bad with people and houses everywhere, but here it's worse.*

*The people are all sandwiched together with their homes are nothing but muddy concrete, metal and scrap wood or straw.*

*We have one colored man named Reggie who lives in a shack outside of town. His place is ten times better than what these people have to live in.*

*From the world tour the military has given me, I think once I get home, I'll just stay put.*

*Forrey*

Charlie chuckled at Forrey's letter, mainly because he himself felt the very same way when he was in the Navy. 'You can take the man out of the small town, but you can't take the small town out of the man.' Charlie leaned back in his chair and wiped the tears from his eyes. His children would say, after they had grown up, that when tears came to their father's eyes he never wiped them away in shame but instead, grateful. The tears acted like a nerve tingling to life, notifying the body that it will soon be using the flaccid limb.

Reginald "Reggie" Jackson, the youngest son of a freed slave, determined in his heart to walk every acre of his nation as a free citizen. It is the Snake River that weaves its feral beauty along the southern stretch of Idaho, and no tropical oasis can compare to the claim the valley holds on the residence of King Hill. When Reggie arrived in King Hill, that claim halted his travels, his exploring days were over, he was home.

His father and grandmother worked on one of the few plantations where the owner insisted everyone, on his plantation, learn to read the Bible. Reggie's grandmother taught him how to read and write. His Father encouraged him to travel his nation, work for his food and never hold a grudge against any man or woman who would only see his color. "Slavery is as old as Adam and Eve." His father used to say, "It's false idealism and false superiority of the human races are not fixed just because one side lost the gun fight."

Though there would always be those who would die in their prejudice, Reggie was well liked in the area. From the first Sunday that Reggie showed up in King Hill, he would always be seen walking to the Baptist Church in Glenns Ferry with his Bible tucked under his arm. He hired on with old man Robertson who had just expanded his farm by another 200 acres and looking for a capable hand when Reggie came to town. Old man Robertson took to Reggie from the first handshake. Reggie was good-natured, quiet, mainly kept to himself, but there is nothing a working man respects more than another working man who is willing to out work him.

The only house old man Robertson could offer Reggie, if you could call it a house, nestled up against the ridge, just below the newly acquired acreage. It was barely bigger than a pump house with gaps in the walls and the roof. The only luxury was the privy that was up against the house like a lean-to. Gaps were plugged up. The wood-burning stove was repaired along with a sink that drained into the privy. It was a shack, but it was home. Old man Robertson went to the county seat and sectioned out a quarter acre, and for the first time since Reggie's ancestors were sold to the Spanish, Reggie was a proud owner of his own land.

# CHAPTER 14

CHARLIE WAS STARTLED AWAKE by the house vibrating from the passing of a freight train. Every muscle and joint scolded this healthy young working man's body for falling asleep in his chair instead of his bed. Wobbling like an old man wracked by arthritis, Charlie discarded his clothes on the floor and groaned as he stretched out in bed. Undoubtedly Avelle woke up, only enough to roll to her other side opposite Charlie, renewing her tears.

No alarm clock could have jolted Charlie and Avelle from their sleep faster than Charlie's youngest brother, Ernie, calling out from the kitchen like a bugle horn.

"Hey, you guys gonna sleep all day! Rise and shine, 'fore I come in with a bucket of water!" Ernie gleefully laughed as he turned to his mother, hoping he would be able to make good on his threat.

"Ernie!" Gladys Brehan scolded her son. "Is that any way to greet your brother and Avelle? Sometimes I think you act more like three years old than thirteen!" Truth was, Ernie always looked for an opportunity to wake up someone the way his parents had a few years ago with his older brother.

Frankie spent an evening partying along the river with some school buddies who had acquired some moonshine in Hammett. A couple hours before dawn, Frankie came home stumbling drunk, falling up the stairs, fell face down on his bed and passed out. Before the cock started to crow, Gladys and C.L went down to the river and filled up a couple of buckets of the early run-off water. The first bucket of water startled Frankie awake, but it was the second bucket in his face that he was just sure that even penguins don't dive in water that cold.

"Get up Frankie!" C.L barked his order to his son. "The ranch doesn't stop or sleep in, just because you had a night of foolishness!"

From that day on, if anyone ever did see Frankie drink, it was never more than one beer, and he never let the cock crow without him up and getting dressed. Ernie, took the lesson to heart, but couldn't help making the threat of a bucket of water his new "good morning."

"Now you kids take your time about getting up, and I'll just get breakfast started. I'll call you when it's ready." Gladys Brehan by virtue of being the first born of her family as well as the first born on a homesteaded ranch in King Hill was known to be a hard worker. Each pregnancy took it's own toll on her metabolism, and by the time Gladys was pregnant with Ernie, she was well overweight by two hundred pounds.

Two months after her fortieth birthday, Gladys knew with all certainty, another Brehan would be born. The Doctor, however, seeing her pregnancy weight never coming off, thought it time for her go to the Hospital in Boise to rule out a growing tumor.

"Besides," the Doctor told her, "your test came back negative. The bunny never died."

With reluctance Gladys checked into St. Luke's Hospital in Boise and was given a room with a view of the Foothills and Table Rock. That night she lay on her bed watching the stars unfold their magnificent presence in the blackness of space. The first out was the North Star along with it's obedient followers. It was as if God himself was looking down on His child patiently beaconing her to speak with Him.

Gladys prayed with a heavy heart to the only one who seemed willing to listen. "Heavenly Father, You know I have a baby growing inside me, and I know I have a baby growing inside me. But the doctors and C.L and just about plum everybody else in this state thinks it's just a tumor. If they cut me open tomorrow, this baby is going to die, and I don't know how to stop them and make them listen to me." Gladys looked to her hands that were folded in her lap, the starch bed sheet and thin blanket, the plain white room that just makes its patient feel that much more sick. "Please spare this baby Lord." Gladys rested her head upon the pillow. "Thanks for listening. In Jesus name, Amen."

As she fell asleep, Gladys dreamed of holding a beautiful baby boy, and everyone around her laughing and C.L passing out cigars. When she awakened in the morning she had a pressing urge to go to the bathroom and called the nurse to help her up. The moment she sat down in the bathroom, a bloody clot the size of a softball made a splash in the toilet. The doctors confirmed that she indeed had had a miscarriage and called off the surgery.

For nine more months, Gladys fought her feelings and the disbelief of her family and friends that she was still pregnant. The day of Ernie's birth was met with everyone standing around laughing and C.L handing out cigars and beaming with joy. Even after Ernie grew up he still said that the reason for him being so ornery is to make up for his twin brother.

"Grandma!" Kath came running out from her bed, and spread her arms across her grandmother's stomach for a hug.

"Good morning, my Angel. Did you sleep well?" Gladys kissed Kath on her head, returning the hug with all the love a grandmother gives.

"Can I get the kids up, Avelle? They're hollerin'." Asked Ernie.

"Yes you may." Answered Avelle. "But you don't need to do that, Ernie."

"Oh, I know I don't, it's just that I want to. What do I put on them?"

"Just whatever you find in the drawers. Kath can show you. Keep being helpful and I'll wish I had you around here every day." Avelle teased from her bed. "Come on Charlie, looks like it's time to get up." Avelle wanted nothing more than to lay back down on her pillow. Not only was her heart still aching, but now it had spread to her whole body along with a creeping and unwelcoming headache.

"Oh, might as well." Charlie groaned as he sat up in bed. "Don't look like there's much chance of getting any more shut-eye around here."

Before Charlie got dressed, he came around the bed to his wife. "Hey, come here." He lifted Avelle to her feet, wrapped his strong arms around her, and kissed her on the forehead. Avelle fought the impulse to pull away, away from the world, away from life. Through the closed door came the sound of voices and the clattering of pots and pans, awaking Avelle's one soothing memory.

Avelle broke the embrace while fixing her eyes on the closed door. "Sure sounds funny to hear someone else preparing breakfast." Shuffling through her clothes unconsciously, Avelle began remembering out loud. "You know, that's practically the only thing I remember about Mama. Hearing her in the kitchen before I got up in the morning. It's louder in the other bedroom, of course."

"Don't it give you kind of a funny feeling to sleep in here where your folks slept?" Charlie questioned Avelle as if the thought had just now occurred to him.

"It did right at first." Avelle answered without blushing. "But it's been okay for a long time now. I don't think of Mama as being in here, just Papa and Aunt Nell." Avelle picked out a pink cotton blouse and a pair of brown peddle pushers, and set them on their bed. "You remember what I told you about what Forrey said. That's what really made me feel uncomfortable, and I don't know, kind of dirty I guess."

"Yeah, I get you. His mistress taking care of his dying wife. Really doesn't paint a pretty picture, does it?"

"The worst part of all of it is that he's just given up living." Avelle sat down on her bed beside her clothes. "He never has looked truly happy, like he did when Mama was alive. But since the accident it's like he's buried himself in a black hole I don't think he will ever get out of."

Charlie, already dressed in a blue and green western shirt, wranglers, with a silver belt buckle, bent down on one knee in front of his wife and took her hands into his, looked into her grief stricken face.

"I am really sorry for you, about Forrey. Don't you give up living either, Princess." Then with a twinkle in his eye, he added. "For what it's worth, in sickness and in health, you are my one and only till the day I die." Tears streamed down Avelle's face and a lump lodged in her throat as she smiled a grateful smile to her husband as Charlie kissed her hands and got up and passed out of the room.

"Good Morning, Ma. Good Morning, Ernie." Greeted Charlie entering the kitchen in an unsuccessful cheery tone.

"Mornin' Charlie," answered Ernie.

"Good Morning, Son." Gladys spoke gently to her son and offered her cheek for a kiss. "Charles Lawrence Brehan, Jr.!" Gladys scolded. "Have you even washed your hands yet this morning?"

"Have to go outside first, Ma." Charlie kissed his mother,

and with a mischievous smile savored his stolen piece of crisp bacon that still held a few bubbles of sizzling fat.

Avelle dried her eyes and forced herself into composure as she came out to greet her family. Giving her mother-in-law a kiss and a "Good Morning," Avelle picked up the hairbrush from the standing shelf in the bathroom/pantry and began to brush her hair, then Kath's, then Chuckie's. Avelle wet her index and middle finger with her tongue to smooth down the barely visible platinum blonde hair on Nancy Ann. Then by natural motherly instinct, she moved to Ernie's tangled blonde mop as he held the chubby baby on his lap and feeding her a bite of bacon.

"Hey! Take it easy! You don't have to take the scalp too, you know! Besides, I already brushed it once this morning." Ernie protested in defense.

"And I suppose you consider that good for a whole day, don't you? Not that it did much good that I can see." Avelle relaxed a bit as she teased Ernie. "What a person really needs is a curry-combs if they intend to accomplish anything with that rat's-nest of yours. But I beg your pardon if I scraped you sensitive little noggin'." And with that she kissed the top of his head and sat down at her seat at the table.

Gladys began talking to Avelle over Ernie's "Ha. Ha." "Avelle, I seem to have cooked up all the bacon. I hope you don't mind?"

"Of course not. That's what I get it for. I don't usually have it weekdays, Charlie, mostly has hot cereal. So I usually buy a pound Saturdays and cook it all Sunday mornings. I just hope you won't starve, is all."

"Oh, we've eaten. We won't want anything." Gladys assured Avelle.

Charlie had just stepped back into the kitchen and gone to the sink to wash his hands vigorously. "I bet a plugged nickel ol' Ernie can stuff in another bite or so."

"You better believe it, Big Bud!" Ernie sang out in agreement.

"Well, when can't he?" After all these years raising boys, it still surprised Gladys at how much they could eat. "Son, I'd be ashamed to eat again so soon, and after all you ate at home, too!"

"No, no, let him eat." Charlie reassured his mother. "I don't think we'd be able to get a bite down Kath and Chuckie unless he sat down with them anyway."

"He's right, Mom. Besides, there's plenty of eggs and toast, if there isn't too much bacon, and another cup of coffee to go around at least. Charlie, if you're through splashing around there, how about being 'Mother's little helper' for once and set the table?"

Charlie turned from the sink and dried his hands on a white and red striped kitchen towel. "Which Mother am I supposed to be the helper of?" Before Charlie had finished his sentence, Avelle had disappeared out of the house.

"She looks just terrible, Charlie!" Gladys compassionately chimed.

Charlie began setting the table. "I know, Ma. She seemed all right and calm at first, and yesterday she just went plumb to pieces."

"Why didn't you call us, Son? We'd of been glad to come and do anything we could, you know that," inserted Gladys. Charlie shook off the motherly tone that bore down on his nerves as an adult.

"I know, Ma. When I walked into the house yesterday, she just blew wide open. Maud said some lady gave her letters Forrey had written, and then the Doc came by to give her a sedative. There really wasn't anything to do."

Gladys was about to ask about the letters when Avelle came back into the house. Charlie began filling plates as they all sat down to eat.

# CHAPTER 15

FARMERS IN AND AROUND King Hill would sell their famous watermelons, cantaloupes, and honeydews as far as 100 miles away. However, King Hill was also famous for a different kind of watermelon. Red and volcanic in nature, they are rocks that range in size from a grape to a prize winning pumpkin. The typical size is that of a watermelon. For over fifty years after the town's charter, anyone entering the town could still read a Sinclair gas station sign which read, '*Free Petrified Watermelons. Take one home to you're mother-in-law.*'

Avelle walked back into the house, looking as though she were carrying a petrified watermelon on her back.

"Why don't you all come out to the ranch this afternoon?" invited Gladys, sitting down to join the children at the table. "Avelle, I've got a wonderful fat hen boiling right now for dumplings."

"I appreciate it, Mom, I do, but I really don't feel like going anyplace. Charlie, why don't you take the kids and go?" Avelle spoke half plea, half demand.

"No, Princess." Charlie responded with determination to stay by her side.

"Why not, I'd like to know!" Avelle's voice reached to almost a scream. "I'm not a baby that can't be left alone for five minutes. Would you feel better to have Maud come over and…"

"Howdy, folks!" Charlie couldn't have welcomed Clarence's interruption more than in that moment. "Didn't mean to burst in on you right at meal time." Clarence marched into the house with a sober mind, like waking out of a fog and facing a beautiful meadow whose blue sky reached to the farthest ends of the earth.

"Hello, Papa. Come have some coffee." Avelle began to get up to serve her father, but he waved her to sit back down as the morning's musical greetings came all at once.

"Good Morning, Clarence" Gladys and Charlie rang out together.

"Morning, Mr. O'Brien." sang out Ernie.

"Grandpa! Grandpa!," the sweetest greetings came from his three grandchildren.

"Now, now. You all go on and finish. I'll just get a cup and sit down here with Chuck." After pouring his coffee and setting it down beside Chuck's plate, Clarence swooped Chuck into his arms and put him on his lap. "How's

Grandpa's big old man?"

"I's awright." Chuck gruffed his answer in a deep voice, which brought a chuckle to everyone.

"Well, Mrs. Brehan, how's the farm keeping' you? Busiest time of year, I reckon." Sober or not, Clarence had the 'gift-of-gab' better than any trainman, or Engineer.

"Yes, it's all we can do just to make it to town for services. C.L hasn't even been to town in months except for the couple hours on Sunday. Not that it bothers him any." Gladys was about to make her complaint of not being able to go to town when Ernie broke in.

"We got the prettiest sorrel colt you ever saw, Mr. O'Brien!" Ernie's eyes revealed the excitement of Christmas morning. "Dad gave her to me, and I'm gonna train her to be a race-horse! She's out of that blood-bay colt you lost to Mr. Poindexter."

Gladys' cheeks flushed as she looked from Avelle to Clarence to Charlie. Charlie quickly thought of an errand.

"Ernie, why don't you go and see if we left any sawdust out when we unloaded ice yesterday? If we did, you can have it."

"Whooppe! It's just what I need for my training ring!" Ernie jumped from his chair.

"C'n I go, too, please Daddy, please?" Chuck pleaded with his father, jumping down from Clarence's lap.

"Can I take Chuck, Charlie?" The two boys looked at each other, and Charlie answered Ernie.

"If you watch. Chuck doesn't know how to watch out for trains."

"May I go, too, Daddy? Please." Kath couldn't stand to be left behind and spoke as sweetly as possible.

"Yes, Peaches. Take your sister, too." Charlie kissed his oldest daughter on the forehead, and then put Nancy Ann on the floor to walk out with Kath. "Remember to watch out for the trains."

"I won't forget. I watch evr' second." Ernie promised and the cousins bounded out the door. "Gee whiz, that sawdust'll be just the thing for my trainin' ring!"

"Don't get dirty, Son!" Gladys hollered after Ernie, but the reminder fell on an empty screen door that had slammed shut.

"The young scamp. Reminds me of Charlie at that age," Clarence chuckled. After taking a sip of coffee, he looked at Gladys. "Though I think he looks more like you than Charlie ever did, or Louie, or young Fred."

"Yes, they all take after their father, especially Louie." Gladys smiled as her heart brought memories of her children when they were all under her care preparing them for life. "You're right. Ernie does look like me. He acts like me, too, I'm sorry to say." With a sigh, her cheeks colored a little. "The other boys never went around making unthinking remarks the way Ernie just did. I declare, I don't know what to say."

"Now, don't you go tryin' to apologize for that young feller!" Clarence assured Gladys with his finger drawn to the air as if to make a speech. "Don't you go to scoldin' him later neither! You and me and evr' body else in these parts knows I gambled away that filly. I wish she was all I've let go of. I'm glad to hear some good came out of her, she's a fine piece of horse-flesh."

"Can we please stop all this talking about the past!? Here, Mom. Papa, have some more coffee! Here, Hon, have the rest of my bacon and eggs. I don't feel hungry." Avelle's prickly tone sent everyone searching for a safer topic.

"Sure." While chewing on the last bite of his meal, Charlie took Avelle's plate and set it on top of his.

"Did you say if you meant to come out or not, Avelle?" Gladys reminded Avelle gently.

"I'm sorry, I just don't feel like it." Avelle answered flatly.

"Baby, Nell sent me over to see if you kids would come to supper about four. She says you can come on over anytime though. She's cooking chicken and noodles." Avelle didn't feel like being around anyone or eating anything, so why was a room full of people not leaving her alone and asking her to eat?

"Papa, tell her I just don't feel up to it today. Mom already asked us out, too, but I'm not up to it."

"Why don't you all go into the front room so I can clear up in here." Gladys began cleaning up the table.

"I should say not! After lying in bed and letting you fix breakfast, I am certainly not going to have you clean up as well!" Avelle objected.

"Come on, Charlie. Why don't you and me go out in the yard and let these gals fight over who's gonna to do most of the work. Women! You don't see men folk fightin' over who gets to wipe dishes clean! Besides, I heard about a good deal you might be interested in." The two men walked out the door.

Like squirrels scampering around a walnut tree gathering nuts, Avelle and Gladys got the house set to rights. With the dishes dried and put away, Avelle followed Gladys outside for the wind and breeze to dry out the dishtowels. Today Avelle brushed to the side the differences in cleaning the breakfast dishes. Today, Gladys endeavored to be helpful without instructing her own ways of housekeeping.

The morning sunlight danced its rays upon Charlie's head and face as he walked up to Avelle hanging the dishtowels.

"Princess, your Dad just told me about a real deal. You know that Vogler kid that went into the Army last week? Well, he just bought a '51 Plymouth, and he left it up to his Dad to sell it for him. They are willin' to take $200 for his equity!"

"How much has he got into it?" Avelle wanted to know.

"He traded in a Ford Coupe, same years as ours, gave Morris $270 down and has paid two payments, all together about $400. What'd you say that would leave owing, Clarence?"

"The way me and the twins figured it out, he's got another $400 to pay off Morris."

"They are willing to sell the car for $600?" Avelle questioned.

"Yeah, like I say, you can't beat the deal, and he didn't have it long enough to hurt it." Clarence added, like a car dealer selling another car.

"You said that Mr. Vogler wants $200 cash and the

purchaser takes over the contract?" Charlie looked at Avelle and then to Clarence, with the eyes of a kid in a candy store for the first time.

"Yeah, the way I get it, the kid left some bills owin' and they're pushin' the old man for them, and he wants to get out from under them. He said he'd already talked to Morris and there won't be any hitch about getting it signed over."

"Want to go in and take a look at it, Princess?"

"What color is it?" Avelle couldn't help but ask.

With wide eyes, shoulders scrunched to his ears and palms out to heaven, Charlie spoke amazedly of the priorities of the female species. "What difference does that make, for crying out loud?"

Clarence intervened, "Its dark green, Baby, white sidewalls, radio and heater. I know you kids will hate yourselves if you can afford it and let it get away. It's just like getting the other $200 free."

Avelle wrestled in her mind the idea of a contract. She could tell Charlie wanted it, but couldn't see how they would ever be able to buy a house if they spent it all now on a car. "I know it sounds like a good deal, but can't we wait a while longer?"

"My truck is all but fallin' to pieces right before our eyes, and if Morris will give me another $200 off, we can't afford not to. It was you that brought up the subject to go to town in Frank's DeSoto the other night, if I remember."

Did I?"

"Yes, you did."

Avelle crossed her arms in front of her. "I don't

remember anything like that!"

"Boy! Would I *ever* like to have your memory! If it don't fit in, forget it! You know Clarence, every time I try to win an argument, I get the same old thing...'I don't remember saying anything like that!'" Charlie squeaked his voice for a dramatic effect. "Now I ask you...Is that any way to win an argument?"

Clarence dared not to defend his son-in-law by explaining his own marital arguments. "You should complain! Nell never gives me a chance to argue. She just goes ahead, and I don't know nothing about it 'till afterwards."

"Yah." Avelle laughed. "How'd ya like it if I did that, Smarty?!"

"Answer me once already! Shall I go in with Clarence and take a look at the Plymouth?"

"Sure won't cost anything to look, *if* that's all you do. Though, I got a hunch it won't stay that way for long." Avelle spun around and headed back inside, the little angel on her shoulder couldn't help but ask, 'Why are you being so salty with Charlie? You know you want a more reliable car.'

"Clarence, if you don't mind waiting a minute, we'll run over to the Vogler's together," Charlie walked over to the icehouse to his mother and children.

Clarence responded with a nod and heavily walked over to the truck and lit up his rolled tobacco while waiting for Charlie.

"Mom, I'm going to run into town with Clarence to look at a car. Can you stay with Avelle till I get back?"

"Why, I suppose so. How long do you think you'll be?"

"No more than a couple hours, I suppose."

"What's wrong with the car?" Gladys didn't even try to hold back her tongue.

"Now, Ma! Is that nice? After all, he still knows people from the old days. Matter of fact, it's his friend's son who owns the car. He enlisted last week and Uncle Sam don't approve of GI's driving their cars, especially during Basic. They like to keep 'em busted and afoot...makes the discipline easier."

"Well, aren't you salty this morning!" Gladys puzzled over her son's change in attitude.

"Thanks, Ma." Charlie kissed his mother on her cheek and headed inside to say goodbye to his wife. When he went into the bedroom, he saw her lying across the bed, crying softly. Lying beside her on his side, Charlie lovingly stroked Avelle's back.

"Here now, Princess, that's no good. Why don't you come into town with your Dad and me?"

It's not that. It's... Oh, Charlie!" Avelle's soft cry turned into heaving sobs.

"What, Honey?" Charlie listened with focused attention, wondering what could have added to his wife's distress.

"I guess I wasn't thinking the other night. The Doctor *told* me not to let myself get upset, and I forgot! And now there's no baby, not anymore! Oh! I feel like a murderer!" Avelle went over again, the Ferris wheel, the roses, the romance, the grief, accusing herself for not coming home right after eating and putting herself in bed. But how could she have just cried a little? It wasn't right to torture herself, she knew that. It was as if the Devil himself stood at the end of her bed laughing at her pain with no pity.

"Now Avelle, that's no way to talk. You'll make yourself sick. Or sicker, anyway. Do you feel sick? Does it hurt much? I won't go to town at all. I'll stay right with you today."

"No, Honey. I feel all crowded up, everything seems to be happening at once. Can we let the kids go home with your mother or something? I feel like I've got to be by myself for a little while. Please don't mind, Darling. It just seems like everything is all of a sudden too much. All I want to do is get back in bed and stay all day." Avelle turned her head to face Charlie. Charlie saw in her eyes the sorrow deep in her soul. The pain Charlie saw hurt more than the loss of a beloved brother-in-law.

"Is that what you really want?"

"Yes." Avelle answered pitifully.

"Well, how about this? Ma can take the kids, and I'll ask Maud to watch the door and see no one comes and bothers you. You know they are going to be coming over any time, the word's out by now."

Avelle's face relaxed at the relief of Charlie's words. "Oh, how wonderful that sounds. Would you mind if I went right to bed and let you talk to your Mother? I feel like if I have to explain this to her, too, I'll come all unstuck again."

"Of course, Princess. Anything you want, you know that." Charlie's face went from compassion to exhortation. "Just try to rest. Remember! This can't have been your fault. It's nobody's fault. It just happened is all! The whole thing's just been more than you could take. There's no guilt or shame in that!"

"You're the best husband a woman could ever ask for." Avelle sat up with Charlie and gave him a tight hug and thankful kiss.

Charlie got up from the bed and gave a dramatic Opera-like bow. "At your service, my queen." Then he picked up her nightdress and draped it over his arm, served it to her and stepped out of the room softly closing the door behind him. A burst of laughter momentarily dried the shed tears as Avelle watched her husband's performance.

# CHAPTER 16

SHE HADN'T BEEN FLAT more than an instant when Charlie shouted something about his mother and ran towards the tracks. Someone else, probably Clarence, ran by the house in his wake. "Oh, no! The children are with Ernie looking at the sawdust!" She jumped out of the covers and ran onto the porch stoop in her nightdress as the warning whistle from an oncoming train pierced the air.

Charlie and Clarence were assisting Gladys with all the children safely away from the tracks when Avelle looked back toward to the ice house.

"I was hurrying to get everyone across before the train came and I stumbled over the rail is all!" Gladys frustratingly explained.

"Are you bad hurt, Ma'am?" Clarence asked with concern.

"No. Just my ankle. Let me go, you two! I can walk fine. Are the kids all safe over?"

"Yes." Charlie had to stop talking until the passenger train roared past. The Engineer waved curiously at the older woman limping between two men, kids jumping and screaming on the lawn above, and a young woman in her night dress on the porch. The passengers also noticed the peculiar show, but missed any glimpse of the young woman on the porch. Avelle caught the Engineer's stare and dashed into the home like a flash of light. Faster than a jack rabbit skips away, the train was gone, whirling dark choking smoke and sawdust aimlessly in its wake.

"You sure you're alright, Ma?" Charlie asked concerned.

"Oh! I'm fine! You two quit treating me like a cripple! Let go! I can walk, I tell you! After all I'm used to falling by now. Or else I'll never be." Gladys hobbled over to her car.

"How did it happen, Ma?"

Leaning against the grill of her car, Gladys rubbed her right knee and calf. "I was hurrying the children across before the train got between. I don't believe they ever heard it. I caught my foot over the rail coming back over is all. Thank heaven I handed Nancy to Ernie to carry, or I would have dropped her, too."

Before Charlie could ask why they were on the other side of the track, Ernie burst his defense. "I did so hear the train! We were gonna sit on that side until it went by. I never seen a train from the river side, before! Now I probably never will!" With Ernie's protest, he kicked at the rocks and dirt that lay as a driveway.

"Don't just stand there, bring her in!" Avelle, draped in Charlie's worn cotton grey robe, was now standing in front of Gladys.

"I'm not hurt, dear. I just need to hurry home before I get stiff." Gladys began to stand up to show she could walk.

"Aren't you gonna stay and watch the kids?" Charlie asked, hoping his mother would still stay.

"Oh, Charlie! Not now!" Avelle protested.

"Oh, I'll be alright, Avelle. Besides, Ernie can watch them, if I can't." Gladys wouldn't let a little fall stop her from helping out.

"Gee whiz! How'll I ever get my training ring made if I got to watch kids?! Holy Cow!" Ernie had no intention of watching his nieces and nephew today.

"Ernie! Watch your language!" scolded Gladys.

"Now, Ernie!" Charlie was about to reprimand his little brother when Clarence broke into the conversation.

"Now, Charlie. Remember how you used to feel when your mom made you watch the younger ones? Why not let them spend the day with Nell? She'd love it, you know. It'd keep her from moping...give her a reason to perk up a little."

Charlie looked at Avelle to see what she thought, but in his mind he thought, "Yeah, like she's got nothing to do but mope."

"Would you mind going over and seeing how she feels, then come back and get them if it's okay?" Avelle pleaded softly.

"Well, there's no reason why I still can't watch the kids! Kath, honey, don't you want to see Ernie's colt again?"

Gladys cared little for the throb of her foot that was beginning to register in her mind.

"I saw it, Grandma, and Ernie won't let us pet it, or get close to it even." The idea of spending the day with Ernie was the last thing Kath wanted to do, too.

"Oh, I do so!" Ernie rolled his eyes at Kath.

"You do not!" Kath stared straight at Ernie with distain.

"Do!"

"Don't!"

"Children!" Reprimanded Gladys. "Honest, Ernie, you don't act any older than Kath sometimes. I better shove off before I get too stiff and need a stretcher to get me home. If Nell doesn't feel up to watching the kids, just bring them to the ranch. You know we are always glad to have them. Come on Ernie, get in." Gladys tried not to appear as though she was hobbling around the car.

"Ernie, tell Dad I'm going to look at a car, a '51 Plymouth. I'll try to get out tonight, there's something I need to talk to him about. Or if Louie shows up, ask him to come in. And, oh, go easy with that colt, fella! Over-training spoils many a fine race horse," Charlie instructed his baby brother.

"Brothers!" Ernie shook his head and slumped into the car.

The young Brehan family and Clarence O'Brien waved Gladys and Ernie goodbye and watched them pull onto the highway driving toward the ranch.

"Your mother falls a good bit for a woman her size, don't she? It's a miracle she wasn't hurt." Clarence observed to Charlie.

"Avelle thinks it's because she feels insecure, or some such thing. Personally, I think she don't pay any attention to where she's going." Charlie turned around to face Avelle and his children.

"Do we get to go play with Teddy and the twins? Do we, Mama?" Kath asked hopefully.

"I suppose so, Honey." Avelle smiled at her daughter, thinking she could see her mother in her daughter's eyes. "Papa, are you sure Aunt Nell would feel like taking care of them today? I mean, I can ask Maud to watch them instead. Tell Aunt Nell I feel all right, just tired, and that I'll walk over after a while." Avelle's voice struggled not to sound lifeless.

"I'm sure. Nell's already expecting you for dinner. A few hours extra isn't gonna matter much," reassured Clarence.

"Okay kids, go get in the car. Here, Clarence, take Nancy Ann." Charlie picked up the baby, who was playing with some rocks. Clarence took the baby from Charlie and helped the children pile into the car. Charlie kissed Avelle goodbye and told her to get some rest, then went to the Warnick's to talk to Maud. Avelle turned into the house and laid back on her bed. Fatigue hit her like a derailed freight train as she again slept with bitter dreams.

Clarence mused at the sixteen month old as she clutched one of the rocks. He loved watching the constant and innocent fascination babies and toddlers have as they discovered their new world. Kath climbed into the backseat, but before Chuckie would climb into the back, he offered to his Grandpa, that maybe he could drive. With a tossle to

Chuckie's hair, Clarence convinced him to wait for his father.

After a few more minutes with everyone seated in the Ford, Charlie opened the driver's door and slid behind the steering wheel. "Here we go, Kath. Remember to help Aunt Nell take care of your sister, and keep Chuckie out of mischief if you can. Your mother will be over after awhile."

"Where are you going, Daddy?" Kath asked, not exactly thrilled for not getting permission to simply play and have fun.

"Your Grandpa and I are going to town, and maybe we'll come back with a new car. Would you like that?" Charlie roared the rattled the engine to life.

"No." Kath answered.

"No?" Charlie looked back at his daughter before preparing to cross the highway.

"I like this car. When we go to town, you and Mama can't hear what me and Chuckie is saying." Kath answered resolutely.

A burst of laughter exploded from Charlie and Clarence as the car went across the highway to the O'Brien's home. The baby crowed at the laughter while clapping her hands. Kath and Chuckie looked at each other in the back seat, wondering why Daddy and Grandpa were laughing, and their secrets now exposed.

# CHAPTER 17

AUNT NELL GREETED THE grandchildren inside her door with an open cookie jar while Clarence and Charlie started toward town.

"By golly, this old Ford sure does make a racket, don't it?" Clarence shouted above the shaking of the engine and the muffler that sounded more like a rusty bugle horn.

"Yeah, I'll say. Sometimes I'm sorry I didn't get a little better one, but I knew I'd be cut off a lot and it was between a car or furniture since we couldn't get both." Charlie offered a silent prayer that he would get back to the train crew with enough work and seniority that he would not be cut off again.

Charlie stopped at the only stop sign in King Hill and looked to the left before pulling onto the highway. Clarence looked both to the right and left to confirm the highway was clear to turn onto.

"You kids sure done well. I like to see a young couple with their heads on square."

"All the credit goes to Avelle. She manages our money so tight, I was a little surprised she even mentioned the notion of getting a new car." A proud smile came to Charlie's face, and the verse, *He who findeth a wife, findeth a good thing*, reverberated in his heart.

"Yeah, Avelle sure ain't the flighty type. Reminds me more of her mother everyday." Clarence looked out at the Section House remembering when he was the foreman and not one cloud marred his clear blue sky.

"You know, we were talking about her mother this morning. Was is cancer, or did they even know?"

"Old Doc never would say, but it had to be that. With her dying so hard, I don't know what else would've acted like that. Every time I step into that house I can smell those damn bandages! I wish to God I could have put her in a hospital sooner, but Old Doc said it wasn't any use." Clarence's voice trailed at the last, looking out his window, letting the wind wipe the tears that struggled from his eyes.

Charlie sensed when they first set off for town that Clarence wanted to talk, and after a few minutes of silence restarted the conversation.

"I don't remember anyone getting completely cut off, didn't the Company just cut everyone back?"

"It started with a ten percent cut, and by the end of the false recovery, everyone was at half days. Medical benefits, pension benefits, and vacation time had all but been suspended with the promise that when the Company started making a profit again, all the benefits would come back."

Charlie broke in before Clarence could continue. "The union had a meeting last week, saying they wanted a vote on going to the Company and demanding full restoration of benefits."

"Good for the union! The Company should be held to their word and take care of its employees. You boys gonna strike?" It gave Clarence pleasure every time he heard that the Company who fired him would be forced to cough up their profits.

"I sure hope not. If they start rehiring the train crew, I want to be the one working, not holding a sign for benefits I can provide for myself. But if the hotheads don't keep their cool, holding signs is the only thing we'll be doing." Charlie looked out and saw the river pulling away from the highway.

"Well, I can respect the wantin' to work. Don't think all the money on God's good earth would have cured Christine anyhow."

"Who was working the lower section when you were here?" Charlie remembered how much he could enjoy his father-in-law during his sober hours.

"Old Smead. He used to drive me nuts! Always hanging around watching when I brought the motor-car in, like I was trespassin' on private property or something." Clarence chuckled at the memories that began dancing in his mind as the wind whipped in from the window.

"Where's Smead now?" Charlie had remembered Frank Davis talking about 'Old Smead' keeping everybody sore about his wife running off and how his son would never amount to anything. Truth was, the men on the upper and lower sections had more respect for his son, Stan, than 'Old Smead' himself.

"He had a heart attack and took a medical. He was living with Ronald and his wife, but now he's livin' on the first section this side of Pocatello. Did you know he asked Nell to marry him, right after she came to work for me?" Clarence moved away from the window and turned to Charlie, as if telling a tale.

"No foolin.? Why, the old goat! He must have been at least twenty-five years older than her," Charlie whistled.

"He said he'd give her baby a name. Nell asked Christine and me about it, and I asked her what was the advantage to a kid having a name like "Smead." She must've told him what I said cause he barely spoke to me from then on." Clarence deeply chuckled.

"Was he around when Avelle's mother died?" Charlie was still puzzled over Clarence's behavior toward Nell.

"No, a month after he made Nell that proposal, Nell's baby ended up dying and two months after that, he up and had the heart attack."

Glenns Ferry seemed quiet and still as Charlie pulled into town. Parishioners parked their vehicles at the various churches, while others were still fast asleep in their beds. Charlie couldn't remember the last time he took his family to church.

June had been an excessively dry month, but one wouldn't know it by the green lawns of the homes and the lush grass that wrapped around the wild-growing sagebrush upon the untouched hills. The farms now fully yielded their bountiful crops.

Charlie continued to reminisce while pushing the quiet invitation to church back into the recess of his mind. "The only thing I remember of the depression is that after we traded off the house and went out on the ranch, feed was a bit scarce, and the hogs we had that first year in the trade ended up being slaughtered 'cuz there was no market for them."

"We sure didn't have it near as bad as those big cities. How come C.L never went back to running an engine?" Clarence couldn't fathom the idea of any man voluntarily giving up one of the best-paying jobs in the county.

"He had the ranch going good by that time. Never did sign back in. Said he liked it better being his own boss. Said the ranch was a lot better place to bring up us kids, too. I'm not sure he's not right. Every time I get cut off, I've half a notion to go in with him. I asked him a couple years ago. Said I'd be welcome but that he bought the place for him to raise his family without expecting his boys to take over." Charlie knew Avelle wouldn't want to live with his mother.

"Just when we'd get to seriously considering the idea, I'd get called back to work," (to the relief of both echoed in Charlie's mind).

"Ain't it awful quick after the baby for you kids to have

another one? Not that I'm buttin' into your business. You seen what that kind of stuff's done to Nell. Avelle looked real bad this morning, too."

The Episcopal Church chimed the half hour, and soon the town would be coming alive with everyone coming out of their homes or out of their worship.

"Well, she cried all night, and this morning she said that she was no longer going to have a baby. We weren't..." Clarence cut off Charlie in surprise.

"What?! Did she miscarry?! Oh, my poor baby!" Clarence's heart stung with grief for his daughter and felt ashamed for butting into her family affairs.

"I guess so. She told me just after we talked about going to Vogler's. Said she wanted to go to bed and rest. I thought about calling the doctor, but she said she just wanted to be left alone." As he passed the streets that lead him to the Vogler's, Charlie debated within himself if he shouldn't stop by the Doctor's.

"She seemed so accepting and resolved Friday night. What got her all busted up?" Clarence grieved at the idea of not being able to wipe his daughter's tears away. He only remembered her crying when her mother died.

"A girl Forrey met in Texas came and brought her some letters he wrote. Mostly, they were about how much he thought of Avelle. When she got them and started reading, she just broke wide open and buried herself in our room."

"I never knew he had a girl? How come she's way up here?" Regret and curiosity filled Clarence at the same time.

"I don't know. I haven't had a chance to talk to Avelle

about it at all, really. This morning was not the time to bring it up. I did go through the letters last night though. Nothing much to them, just what you would expect from a homesick boy. She cried so hard that I about phoned the Doc." Charlie remembered all the letters that he wrote to Avelle after they had met. Avelle still kept them in a treasure box in the closet. Charlie knew that Avelle would keep the letters from Forrey in a treasure box, too. "But just as I was about to call him, he showed up with an unexpected house call to check on her."

"That bad, huh?"

"Yeah, and it must've been an hour after the sedative before she finally quieted down. I sat up in the front room for most of the night. She just kept moaning and crying in her sleep."

"I know it might sound heartless, but you ought to be glad she finally broke down. I seen a couple of women...well you take Nell...when her baby died. If she ever shed one tear, I never knew it. When it don't come all out at first, it just seems to change 'em completely. I don't know when I've ever seen her really laugh since." Clarence shook his head with empathy as they pulled onto the block where the Vogler's lived.

"Do you think Nell's bottling up had more to do with all the troubles she had growing up?" Charlie remembered Avelle telling him about her and Forrey's last conversation.

"No, she took it all good-natured-like. But when her baby died, I thought she was pretty cold. I know it's still on her mind 'cuz she brought it up yesterday morning. Said she remembered how Forrey took to the poor little tyke."

As they pulled up to the Vogler's, Charlie turned off the engine, their ears still ringing from the rattling engine and muffler. Charlie wondered how Clarence could justify his relations with Nell with all she had been through and with his wife dying under the same roof. Clarence sensed his son-in-law's thoughts and kept the both of them in the front seat as he defended himself.

"No man who's never had trouble knows what pushed a man who has. Someday when you got nothing to do, just wonder a little how you'd like to be married to a woman you don't love and never did, and have a big brawlin' bunch of kids you can't support! I ain't complaining. I made my bed and by God I'll lay in it! And none of your's or Forrey's talk of grace can fix the wrong I done either! But don't you go thinking, too, that every woman is perfect just 'cuz yours is! The light went out for me when Christine died, and I'd been a better man if I'd blowed my brains out right then. I suppose I had some noble idea of saving myself for my kids. Well, you see how that turned out." Clarence's face lightened at every sentence, like he had a harness strapped to his shoulders straining to pull out a stump by himself.

"Now, Clarence, there's no reason to go on like that!" Charlie puzzled over Clarence's adamant defense. When did Forrey ever talk to his father about God's grace?

"Oh, hell, I guess you're right. If I keep flappin' my yap, I'll be bawlin' on your shoulder. Son, let's car-deal!"

# CHAPTER 18

THE TWO MEN CLIMBED out of the Ford and were greeted by two excitable teenagers. Marge and Connie had seen Charlie's Ford parked in front of the house and agreed upon a sufficient protest of why they shouldn't have to go home. Barely had they begun to shout, beg, and plead when Old Vogler broke their racket by informing Charlie and Clarence that the Plymouth was parked in the detached garage at the rear of the property. The men disappeared around the house as the teenage girls stood with their mouth's gaping. They huffed and puffed at the insult of being ignored and went back into the house.

Just as Cain and Abel debated and fought over the best sacrifice, through the generations of time it has varied little: The best stone club maker, the best horse breeder, the best

Gladiator, or the best sports team, man's one debate that will stand the test of time is the best vehicle manufacturer: Buick? Chevy? Dodge? Ford? GM? Plymouth? Their idle conversation does not rest in women, politics, or religion. It most certainly begins with work problems and ends with cars. All of life's problems could be solved if we would just look to the example of the smooth-running performance of a motor vehicle and its relative parts.

Charlie, Clarence, and Vogler had not long been under the hood of the Plymouth when Vogler's neighbors, Doug Starlett and Brian Metcalf, espied Charlie's car and drifted over. Doug and Brian were Section Hands in Glenns Ferry, and like Charlie, waiting to be hired back on as Firemen and Brakeman.

In another fifty years the training and education to become an Engineer or Conductor would come through university courses or technology classes. For now, however, it was on the job training. The Engineers were to train the fireman. The Conductors were to train the brakeman.

"You finally gonna get rid of that rattling cage on wheels, Charlie?", teased Doug.

"Yeah. She's been a good rig, but she just doesn't have it in her anymore," Charlie spoke with regret.

"Goin' from a Ford to a Plymouth, huh? It's a pretty thing, but you're not exactly trading up now are ya?" For Doug, there was no sense getting anything other than a Chevy.

"Watch it there, Son. I'm trying to car-deal." Old Vogler always liked a good car show-down, but not while he was trying to sell his son's Plymouth.

"Have you heard D.J say anything about getting us back on?" Charlie wisely turned the conversation, and the men who previously had their heads under the hood now stood erect.

"He said another two weeks to a month. He don't look for us to be cut off at all next year, either," answered Doug.

"Boy, I needed that bit of good news." Charlie was grateful to be working the Section, but he had been itching to get back on the train crew.

"Doug here is already lined up to get his first call back tomorrow." Brian teased.

Doug turned to Charlie teasing with some seniority banter. "You know if you would have signed up and not gone into the Navy, you'd already be an Engineer."

"Duty before pleasure, Starlett. Duty before pleasure." Charlie retorted.

"How's Avelle doing, Charlie? Maggie and Connie haven't really talked about it that much." Vogler did not get much out of Clarence either.

"What are you talking about, Vogler?" Doug asked what seemed to be on the visitor's mind.

"Her brother got killed. You know Forrey." Charlie was surprised that none of the men that had walked up that afternoon had heard the painful news.

"When did it happen?", one of them spoke up.

"She got the news Friday. All we know is what the telegram said, and it didn't say much." Charlie began to explain.

"He was overseas?" Brian was shocked he never heard that Forrey had even enlisted.

"Yeah, said that he got killed near Seoul, some little place, I never heard the name before." Charlie thought that even if he had heard the name, seeing it on paper, he'd never figure out how to pronounce it.

"He fixed my car for free the last time he was on leave. He sure looked good. I told him to stay out of the way of them bullets, and he said they'd have to run over him with a locomotive to do him in." Doug sighed and looked out at the street as some boys rode their bikes at full speed heading to some planned mischief.

"Well, I better get home and tell Marie. Does Avelle feel like seeing anybody? Marie will want to go out and see Avelle." Doug was a freshman in high school when Forrey graduated and had always looked up to him.

"Best to give her another day or so. She took it kind of funny...never said a word about it...neither Friday or Saturday morning. Then when I came home after lunch, she was laying down in bed, bawling her heart out." While Charlie explained to Doug about his wife's grief, the men listened with heads bowed and hands in their pockets. "I don't think she slept hardly two hours last night. Once I take this baby for a little spin, I got to get back, too. I wouldn't have come off to town, except she said she wanted to be left alone. Give her another day, and she'll be in better spirits."

"Charlie, why don't we fire her up, and you can take her around town?" Vogler dropped the hood and started the Plymouth's engine.

"We'll make sure we come out this week, Charlie. Brian, you ready to go?" Doug and Brian headed off as Charlie climbed into the Plymouth for a test-drive. Vogler's neighbors stood around and talked a while longer and were gone by the time Charlie got back.

The only indication to Charlie that the engine was truly running was the acceleration when he applied the gas pedal. He chuckled about how use to the rattling of his Ford he had become. Now he would not only be able to hear the conversation of his children in the backseat, but the conversation of anyone in any car next to him. 'Maybe now,' he thought, 'Avelle will finally agree to learn how to drive.'

As Charlie winded the streets of Glenns Ferry, his thoughts turned from the reliability of the car's engine and the comfortable drive to a home and finally working the job he had been dreaming about since he was a boy. Turning the Plymouth back toward Vogler's, Charlie saw a white-headed man, slightly overweight with a perfect posture, strolling down the road with a naked willow branch in one hand.

Mr. Forbes was the engineer Charlie had taken his student trips with...one of the best. He was known, loved, and respected not only in the town but also wherever his train took him. He treated the students and young qualified firemen as intelligent human beings instead of subnormal animals, as some of the other 'old heads' did. Charlie pulled off the road, eager to speak with his mentor and friend.

"Howdy, Mr. Forbes."

"Oh, hello, Son. What are you doing in town?" Mr. Forbes stopped immediately from his walk and bent down to the passenger window.

"Came in to see about this-here car Vogler wants to sell." Charlie turned off the engine and got out to a proper handshake.

"Oh, yes. Is this it? What's he asking for it?" Mr. Forbes stroked the hood of the car as if to know the engine that lay inside.

"$200 and pay off Morris," Charlie answered happily.

"Pretty good. Are you going to take it?" Mr. Forbes took his eyes off the car and looked at Charlie.

"Most likely. I want Avelle to see it first."

"I'm sorry to hear about Forrey. Make sure you give Avelle my condolences. Did she take it pretty hard?" Mr. Forbes asked with concern.

"Yeah, she feels bad, real bad. She was determined to be alone for awhile today. I figured it was best to let her have some peace and quiet and get it all sorted out." For a moment Charlie felt himself somewhere between wanting to be away from the world and being a shield for his wife.

"Did you hear that D.J put seven men back on Monday? That leaves it right down to you and another four to eight men. I suppose you have a place lined up to live in." Mr. Forbes had a knack for testing the lake of conversation to see if any fish were biting before posing any straight forward question.

"Yeah, Doug Starlett stopped while I was at the Vogler's place and said it looked like we would get back soon. As far as a place goes, I'd like to hold the section house as long as I can. We've almost got a real pretty down payment saved. Do you know of any places for sale?" Charlie knew that Mr. Forbes would be the one to ask.

"What are you looking for?"

"A small house, three to four rooms, on a big lot. I can carpenter, you know, and I'd sooner buy a run-down place and pay it right off and remodel it to suit myself than be paying off a place all of my working days." Charlie thought about some of the lots he had seen that day, though none had a 'for sale' sign. Not that it would have made any difference, homes were sold because someone moved away or died. The city council never voted to approve new building permits which kept the one realtor's office about as quiet as the morgue.

"I think I know of someone willing to sell. Can you pay as much as $500 down?"

"Yeah, easy. We have better than $2,000 saved." Charlie felt the pride of Avelle's hard work of saving now ripe for the gleaning.

"Really! You surprise me. I don't know when I've heard of a man holding his savings while he was cut off." Mr. Forbes learned something new that solidified his good opinion of this young Fireman.

"I can't take all the credit; it's Avelle's idea. She hates like poison to pay rent, and the only way we'll ever have enough for a down payment is for her to save. And then we aren't paying any rent out there." Charlie knew Avelle would be blushing even though the compliment was true.

"How did you get on over there when you get cut off each year?" Mr. Forbes knew better than anyone else how difficult it was to get work anywhere let alone on the Section, especially for those men who were at the bottom of the seniority.

"Must be Providence. I can't explain it. Each time I get cut off the rails, a spot on the Section opens up, and old Davis doesn't want the house." Charlie did his best to live the way the Bible taught, whether he got blessed by it or not. Charlie couldn't help but smile because it sure was nice to give the credit to God when there was no other explanation.

"I thought he was pretty ornery. How did he come to let you have the house?" Mr. Forbes kept probing Charlie for some reason besides Providence.

"We were living in my old apartment, and I was driving back and forth. Well, everyday I was a little late, so he asked me why I didn't move out. I said I would if I knew where I could get a place. So every year since, we've lived in his house. He says I can have it as long as I want it. He's not too bad. He reminds me of one of my Chiefs in the Navy." Charlie mused. "Well, I best take this car back and get home to Avelle before anyone gets the idea I've skipped town."

"Before you go, Charlie, I want to talk to you about something I saw while passing your folk's ranch yesterday."

"Oh, yeah?"

"I saw a man duck into that cave with that little sandy beach. I don't know if I spooked him with my whistle for the crossing but he left a blue shirt hanging over a sagebrush. Does your dad have a new hired hand?" Cecil Forbes had seen a lot of hobos and vagrants hiding in boxcars and rock shelters along the river over his thirty years of being an

Engineer. In the cab of the Engine there is little to do but talk and observe God's beauty along the rails.

"This morning I had Ernie tell Dad I wanted to talk to him about that same thing. The other day I saw some footprints around that same cave. I'll go over there tonight and talk to him about it. Thanks for having your eyes open for me."

"No problem. You kids stop by next time you're in. So long." With a handshake goodbye and a wave, Mr. Forbes headed home from his stroll and Charlie made a straight path back to Voglers.

Vogler and Clarence were sitting outside on the back porch drinking some sun tea when Charlie pulled the Plymouth into the garage. All three men met at the trunk.

"So how'd ya like it?" Vogler first asked.

"Quiet. A couple of times I wasn't sure it was running." All three men chuckled.

"You gonna take it?" Vogler asked.

"I still have to talk it over with Avelle. Do you mind if we come out tomorrow night?"

"That's fine, just fine. If she likes it, you can just give me the cash and then go sign with Morris. Is that all right by you?" Vogler walked Charlie and Clarence to the Ford.

"Sounds good. I'll see you then." Charlie and Clarence climbed into the Ford and with a wave good bye, shoved off.

On the way back, the two men were uneasily quiet. They were like two men getting ready for a duel, back to back, twenty paces apart, and neither one wanting to turn around. It surprised Charlie that he hadn't seen his father-in-law drink one drop all day, nor ask to be taken to the store or the bar. Charlie's mind was also full of the conversations he had had that day, and who was Mr. Forbes speaking of whose owners would take a $500 down payment?

Clarence, for the first time in a long time, didn't want a drink, which was a perplexing notion. His favorite tune, 'My Wild Irish Rose' hummed in his mind and escaped through his throat. He wanted to tell Charlie about the letter he got from Forrey just yesterday, but couldn't formulate the words to talk about it.

# CHAPTER 19

NELL'S IMPATIENCE WAS SWELLING by the time Charlie and Clarence walked back in the door. Outside the walls of the kitchen, it sounded like an angry beehive rather than twelve hungry children and dinner nearing completion. Nora was already feeding Nancy Ann and Freddie and Fae were busily setting the table. Constant shouts of: "I'm hungry!" "I want to sit by Kath!" "No, Me!" "Mom, can I have some milk?" "I want a roll" filled every crack of plaster in the walls.

"Finally! The kids are starving! Did you finish your business, Charlie? Before you sit down, will you please go ask Avelle to come eat? I almost fed the children without any of you." Nell struggled to get her voice above the children.

"Isn't she here yet? I thought she would have been here

hours ago!" Charlie was so used to walking the four blocks from his in-law's to his home that he completely passed the Jalopy. Charlie walked across the highway, his eyes fixed on the door of his home, while his feet carried him to the Warnick's.

Charlie knew he needed to get his wife and that it was time for Avelle to face the family and friends that sympathized with her loss. But how can the chair where the beloved one sat be filled? How is one to finish a puzzle when pieces are lost? What tool is to be used to mend a broken heart? What can prevent grief from the infection of bitterness and anger? Love, patience, and time is the only poultice recipe that can be applied.

As Charlie lead his wife from the Warnick's to the O'Brien's that Sunday in June, he spoke of the car, the possibility of being recalled to active duty, and Mr. Forbes' promise to speak to the owner of a potential permanent home. Avelle anchored herself in Charlie's hand as she listened to him speak.

Though she had been listening to Aunt Nell talking about Forrey's insurance claim, the warming yellow glow of the kerosene lamp began penetrating Avelle's senses like the sun dissipates the misty morning fog. The memory of Forrey's last leave was ending in her mind. He would never again be as vivid to her as he was in that moment. What a marvel the human mind is! It's where one's body can sit at a table listening to the conversation around them while the registering emotions transport them to another time and dimension.

Nancy Ann slept content in Aunt Nell's arms. However, in Avelle's mind, Chuckie was the baby and she hadn't just miscarried, but instead in her womb Nancy Ann grew. Where Forrey's body was not empty of his soul a half a world away, but rather he was sitting with them in the O'Brien's kitchen, laughing and full of joy.

"Forrey never saw her. I wanted him to see how much she looks like me." Avelle whispered with a hint of strength as she took her baby girl from Aunt Nell and placed her on the davenport in the front room.

"That's right. He didn't, did he?" Avelle heard Aunt Nell respond in the kitchen.

The entire day, Nell had been rehearsing what she would say to Avelle and Charlie. For the first time in Nell's life, she had a dream, and the purchase of that dream had come at a costly sum. By the death of her stepson, she was given the chance to rise from the bitter pit of poverty. Nell's eyes focused on Avelle returning to the table. Here were the two she needed desperately to be on her side. All of Nell's words seemed to run like a locomotive traveling downhill with the blind hope there would be a peaceful valley below to catch her.

"I don't mean to cause no more bother than I can help but I don't see no help for it. I ain't used to planning what I'm gonna do with money ahead of time, except for grub and clothes. I've been figuring all day how I could get you two alone, and I almost gave up doing it today. I hoped Clarence would've stayed in town." Nell took a deep breath as she plunged into her proposal.

"Well, here we are...so I'll tell you what I had in mind. Last month, Jimmy took me down to the county seat and I met a Mrs. Steinmetz in the office. Well, we got to talkin' about the rooming house she owns with her husband. Anyway, she said she bet I could run it. After the practice I had with the kids, I bet I could, too!

She said her husband wanted to sell out. He's got arthritis something awful, and he wants to go to Arizona. Ever since, I been wishin' I could lay hands on enough money to buy it. I bet I've thought about it a million times. There's the Base, right there! All those soldiers wanting a room for their wives! Oh, I know I couldn't cut it if I let too many families in, but I can be downright mean when I have to."

Charlie finished his plate, placing it to the side, cautiously focusing on every word. Nell first looked at Avelle, then Charlie, and harnessed her fear of opposition as she justified her intention.

"But I've thought and thought where could I get the money? Or maybe see if she would take a down payment on it and the rest in payments. I even wrote to my cousin in Illinois to see if I could borrow it from him, but I haven't heard nothing yet. But now, if you think it's all right, I'd like to ask her about it, at least, and see if they really want to sell." Nell looked on the young couple, like a cat watching a mouse, ready to pounce against any resistance.

The young couple looked at each other in confusion,

then Charlie questioned unemotionally. "You mean you want to put the insurance money into a rooming house?"

"Well, yes! What's wrong with rooming houses?! I got to do something I know about, you know that! I sure don't have any high flutin' picture of myself as some big hotel owner. But a rooming house, why that's not much different than right here, you know. I thought I'd pay the older girls to help me; they'll be glad of the money, I know."

"Have you asked all the girls about it?" Charlie saw desperation in the tears Aunt Nell fought back.

"No, course not. Until this minute, nobody but me knew what I had in mind. I wanted to ask you and Avelle what, if anything, Forrey had said about his money. He told me before he shipped off that he'd made it out to me'n Clarence. Forrey said that I was to see it was used for the kids, just like the allotment checks." Nell's attention turned to Avelle. She sensed the feared opposition was not as great as she thought, but was bound and determined not to let them leave her home without them wholly on her side.

Avelle could feel Forrey whispering to her heart, "She's never asked for anything, she's never complained, she's never been given a break." Then a long unheard, quieter voice spoke, "She needs your help and support." Avelle spoke up with trepid assurance.

"That's what he told me, too. That's almost the same words. I don't think he ever said anything to Charlie. But we talked about it before he left the last time, and that's what he said the money was to be used for…the kids. Though I don't think he would object."

"For the *kids*, that's the whole thing! Now if I just used it to live on, why the youngest ones would get the short end of the stick. There'd be money to fling around for a while, but then it'd be gone and there wouldn't be anything to gain! That's what I been thinking of. I don't know what he meant I should do! I can't see no way out except to invest it so that everyone comes out equal."

"There's plenty of time to think it over, Aunt Nell. It's kind of a new idea to us, and like you said, to everyone else, too." Charlie was willing to give Nell his stamp of approval, but not without careful examination of the realities of running a business for the first time.

"That's what I thought, too. But yesterday I was in the store and Mrs. Anderson came in with some eggs. Well, I was talking to Bix and just puzzlin' over what we'd do until the insurance came through. The good Lord knows we just been scrapin' by, and what we're to do now that the allotment will stop, well..."

"What did Mrs. Anderson say?" Avelle was in no mood to hear Aunt Nell ramble on, complaining to everyone in town about how bad they have it.

"Well, I was comin' to that. Bix asked me how long it'd be before the money came through, and I said I had no idea...six months or maybe a year. Then Mrs. Anderson apologized for buttin' in. She said when her boy...what's his name, Charlie...the one that was killed in Germany?"

"Ronny. He was a tail gunner in a B29, and the flack killed him *over* Bremerhaven." Charlie added his bit to the memory of a classmate, a little angered to see how quickly the right story is forgotten.

"Oh, yes. Well...she said no, her boy's money came through in about three months. That was right durin' the war, too. Then she said now they don't pay it all in a lump anymore, but in installments."

"You don't say. When did that start in?" Charlie asked a little surprised.

"This April, I think she said. But that don't matter right now. I got to know before Clarence comes back cause if it's just an idea of mine, he'll be against it from start to finish. But if he thinks you kids are for it, why he'll buckle right down. So what do you think? Should I go over tomorrow and see what she'll take for a down payment?" Nell relaxed in her chair, confident she had won her opposition over.

"You've thought about it? You're sure?" Charlie began his interrogation.

"I've thought till I'm most crazy! Do you see any reason why I couldn't run it all right?" Nell fumed.

"I don't know anything about it, but there's got to be more to it than just cleaning up after people. It seems like an awful lot of work. Do you think you could hold up under it? Do you know everything it's going to take to running the place?"

"It's no more different than what I got here! Well, I've got the four twins! Besides, Mrs. Steinmetz must hold up. Her husband can't be too much help, if he's got arthritis as bad as she says."

"She wants to sell for that very reason. She can't run it alone. You can figure that out. Is the rooming house making a profit? Can you be sure that you will be able to get a good return on this investment? Or is it killing her off, and she just wants out?" Charlie wanted to make sure Aunt Nell had looked at the whole picture, not just the idea of a dream.

"Well, if it kills me, it kills me! It's killing me already, trying to figure out how to get the money to raise these kids! I'm sick to death of takin' Forrey's allotment, and now *this*. Forrey's gone! Maybe you think I like takin' the insurance money! He should have had kids of his own to leave it to! He might have, but it cost him every cent he made to feed my kids! I'll never forget that one minute the rest of my life, if I live to be a hundred!" Nell slowly rose from her chair with every sentence. Nell would make every sentence count to prove her case, like a defendant on trial for her life.

"What's the work of a rooming house to me? What's the use of anybody living, if they got to depend on boys like Forrey getting killed to support them? That's blood money! He gave up his living money, now he gives up his blood money to get my kids started! You think a little work's gonna stop me after that?"

Nell's hands were clutched upon the table as she seated herself in the same manner in which she rose, waiting for the pronouncement of her sentence. A brave speech by a brave lady. No one would now dare to doubt that she could run that rooming house in honor of her stepson. She would live for him, as he had died for her.

Something in the way Aunt Nell defended herself made Avelle want to burst into laughing hysterics. Maybe it was surprise, or maybe it was the need to laugh since she had spent the better part of the day crying.

"What do you want us to do?" Charlie reached his hand across the table to Aunt Nell's still clutched hands and gave them a reassuring squeeze. Aunt Nell could feel the tight straightjacket she had wrapped herself in begin to loosen and fall to the side.

"Can you lay off tomorrow and go to Mountain Home with me? That's the best plan I can think of. If she sees I got a man to back me up, maybe she'll deal quicker. I don't like to have to ask you, but I would feel better if I had it set before Clarence found out."

Charlie's eyes sparkled with the humor of remembering the conversation he had earlier that day with Avelle. Clarence had said, "*You should complain. Nell never gives me a chance to argue. She just goes ahead, and I don't know nothing about it 'till afterwards.*"

"I reckon I could get off. I'll go see Davis right away. Coming, Princess?" Both of them had become so used to having both sets of parents living so close, the O' Brien clan leaving would be a definite adjustment for their family as well.

"Yes. Unless you're sure you don't want me to help clear up?" Avelle mumbled a little relieved to be getting up from the conversation.

"No, No. You kids go do what you need to do, and I'll fetch up the other children."

Seeing Nancy Ann still quietly sleeping, Charlie and Avelle stepped out into another clear dark night with its spangled stars and crescent moon. Once a block away, Avelle could hold her laughter no longer. Aunt Nell had made no joke and no hilarity to the conversation. Why then did she laugh? There was no absurdity in the plea Aunt Nell made, nor in the bold manner in which she spoke. But the dark clouds part and the sun comes out to shine. The life that was well loved is remembered, like the perennial flower unfolding with each sunrise, or like the sunflower refusing to give up the sun's fullest rays. Laughter pours its healing honey over the grieving heart, the sweetness soothing the bitterness.

With their composure returned, Charlie and Avelle approached the home of Bix Brunnell. Davis just reached the front door from the opposite direction of the young couple with a half-gallon box of Pecan Brittle ice cream.

"How do, Charlie, Avelle? What brings you over here this late?" Davis tipped his chocolate Stetson Hat.

"That ice cream in your hand there." Charlie teased.

"Charlie!" Avelle scolded.

"No, seriously boss, I need to lay off tomorrow. Aunt Nell wants me to take her to Mountain Home."

"Sure. No problem. That is, if you two come in and sit awhile."

Bix and Susann Brunnell were just finishing up dinner, and Avelle found it of little good to protest the invitation. In a moment they found themselves seated on the wide old-fashioned porch. Each held their blue bowls of ice cream accompanied by three round wafer cookies, and matching mugs placed nearby filled with strong scalded coffee.

The Brunnell's took Davis in like a brother, though

Susann treated both Bix and Davis more like sons. Susann was ten years the senior to both Bix and Davis, and the elderly jokes and playful manner of 'respecting your elders' knew no bounds. It's a small wonder that Davis preferred this childless couple, who at times behaved like children themselves, to the lonely bachelor establishment on Railroad Row.

Charlie and Avelle were given front row seats, as Susann rose and brought Bix his trumpet and Davis his sax. With the skillful spirit of Al Hirt and Louie Armstrong, these two friends would fill the town of King Hill and its valley with tunes like 'Tennessee Waltz,' 'Gypsy in My Soul,' 'Out of Nowhere,' 'Willow Weep for Me,' 'Stella by Starlight,' and various others. No matter what medley they would play, they finished like a prayer with 'Amazing Grace.' No one ever dared complain, however late the hour these two would play, not even Old Gus (if he were ever close enough to hear). It was as if their playful music that seemed to always end in a lullaby would sing the residents into a blissful slumber.

Tonight, Charlie held Avelle close as Avelle quietly dabbed her tears with Charlie's red handkerchief, letting the music sooth her aching soul. After the last note played into the night air, Bix and Davis reverently lowered their instruments to honor the boy their town had lost. They all sat in prayerful silence.

"Well, if I'm going to be rid of you tomorrow, guess I'll go get my rest so I can be in shape to enjoy the peace and quiet." Davis yawned and stretched, ending the private memorial service.

"Oh go on, Boss. You're just thinking of how all the rest of you will have to work twice as hard to make up for me." Charlie continued the jest.

"Say, I hate to bring this up, believe me. Mrs. O'Brien was in yesterday..." Bix sat uneasily as Susann took the Trumpet and Sax inside.

"Yeah, she told us all about it tonight. I had no idea they'd pay the insurance so soon." Charlie removed his arm from around Avelle and leaned toward Bix, as if talking a businessman's secret.

"That Mrs. Anderson, she keeps a close track on what goes on. I just wondered if they was pretty pushed. I'd just as soon give them credit. That Mrs. O'Brien is a pretty good old gal. I offered her credit once before and she'd a like to have taken my head off. She said that the insurance money coming was made out to her?" Bix spoke as if puzzled from the information, not mishandling of funds.

"That's right...or rather to Clarence...but the understanding is that it goes to raising the kids," Charlie confirmed.

"I understand. Well, you let her know I'm good for the grub. How she keeps that bunch of kids fed and clothed is a miracle to me!"

"I'll tell her, but it'll probably be a day or so anyway before she knows what she will do. That's what I laid off for...to take her to Mountain Home on business."

"I see. Well, you tell her what I said."

The three men rose and shook hands, and Avelle thanked Susann for the hospitality. Charlie and Avelle stepped off the porch and made it no more than halfway back to the O'Brien home when a car honked madly and sped past them. The two looked at each other confused and curious when it screeched to a stop at the once intended hotel.

"Well! Who on earth?" Avelle exclaimed then answering in unison with Charlie.

"Louie!"

"Of course! Come on, Princess." Charlie caught his wife's hand, urging her to race. They drew up laughing and panting by the car as Louie stepped out.

# CHAPTER 20

LOUIE BREHAN STOOD IN front of his new 1952 midnight blue Mercury two-door sport coupe. Draped in expense with his grey waistcoat, jacket and hat, he almost seemed displaced from the little town where he had grown up. Avelle mused that if Louie would shave his mustache, he could easily be mistaken for a redheaded Gregory Peck.

"Hmm, Dr. Livingstone, I presume?" Charlie inflected a timely accent when his brother's appearance instantly brought to mind the famous missionary and his rags to riches story. Louie would not stand for his brother's little game to go unanswered and the two brothers inaccurately played out the famous African meeting.

"Well, Stanley, old chap! Fancy meeting you here! Care for a game of cricket, old man?"

"Old man? I dare say, Livy, you are more than five years my senior. And who might this charming lass be?"

"Ah, yes. Allow me to present Mrs. King Hill of 1952."

"Dr. Livingstone." Avelle gave a regal curtsey, then offered her hand for Louie to kiss. All three laughed with the laughter of old friends.

"Did Ernie tell you I wanted to see you?" Charlie wondered if Ernie relayed his message just to Louie or also to their dad.

"No, I haven't seen him. Ernie was out in the barn with the colt the whole time I was home. It was mom that sent me in to see if Avelle could come and stay with her for a few days. Doc says she's got to stay off that leg."

"Doc?! Then she was hurt." Charlie confirmed what he already knew that morning.

"Yes, well, she got home but couldn't make it inside so she sent Ernie in to call Doc. He said the knee was dislocated and her ankle sprained. She sure is miserable."

"I guess there goes my idea of going to Mountain Home with you and Aunt Nell tomorrow," Avelle resigned.

"She wanted to ask if you'd come tonight, Avelle. Dad had to go to Gooding and still wasn't back when I left to go hunt you two up. I don't think any of them have eaten, either. *I'm* certainly not going to cook. It just doesn't seem right."

"Why don't I just come over in the morning, Louie? Besides, I don't think Charlie remembers how to get himself dressed and out of bed, let alone cook breakfast for himself." Avelle teased as she nudged her shoulder into Charlie's chest.

"I'd have you know, I don't need any woman to look after me." Then Charlie strutted his chest and said, "It's a privilege."

"Well, I'll just take my *privileged* self inside and go get our *privileged* children and tell Aunt Nell how *privileged* she will be in the morning to make you breakfast!" Avelle flipped herself from Charlie's embrace and walked into the house, appearing more angry than she truly felt. Charlie watched her go, as Louie whistled a shameful tune.

"Oh, what do you know. Come on and help me get the kids and Avelle home and packed."

To Avelle's surprise, both sets of twins were busy in the task of dinner dishes. Nora and Dora were at the sink washing and rinsing. Timmy finished clearing and wiping the table while Jimmy dried the dishes and placed them back on their shelves. Aunt Nell promised to send one of the kids to rouse Charlie when breakfast was ready. The three sleepy Brehan children were bundled into Louie's Mercury and with Charlie and Avelle in the Jalopy, they set out to stop by home to pack, perhaps for a week.

"I'll come out to the Ranch after I get done with your Aunt Nell. Will you pack me some clothes?" Avelle knew that was about as good of an apology as she was going to get.

"Sure." Then giving her husband a quick kiss, headed inside to pack.

Louie got out of his Mercury and lit a Marlboro he had shaken from the pack. Knowing it wouldn't do any good to offer Charlie one, Louie stuck the pack back into his jacket pocket.

"Before Avelle gets back out here, I need to talk to you about something, especially since I haven't talked to Dad, and Avelle and the kids will be out there tonight."

"What's this about? Or can't you be without your wife for one whole night?"

"Oh, for crying out loud! This is important!" Charlie tried not to yell, but had grown tired of his brother's humor.

"Boy, Mom was right when she said you were salty today."

"Do you want to hear what I got to say or not?"

Holding the cigarette in the corner of his mouth, Louie bowed with his right hand over his heart. "I'm all ears, Captain Barnacle."

Charlie shook his head and began relaying his information. "The day before yesterday we were walking our usual inspection near the ranch. I noticed right at Dead Horse Curve, the sunlight was hitting a spot on that little cave in the choke cherry bush. You know where the ditch empties into the river?" Charlie had gotten Louie's full attention. His brother didn't interrupt but merely nodded his head, understanding Charlie's every word.

"Well, there were footprints all around the cave and at first I thought Ernie must have been just playing around. But as we walked back to the Roundhouse, I thought I saw a man out on the sand, washing his face. Then today I ran into Mr. Forbes and he said he saw a man's blue shirt drying on the bush just outside that cave."

"Have you called the sheriff already?" Louie always knew that spot would be a good hideout. In fact, it was a perfect place for boys to play 'cowboys and indians' when the river was low.

"Not yet. That's why I wanted to talk with Dad. I don't want any bum hanging around out there, and especially now with Avelle and the kids going out. Maybe now that you're here we can go down and look it over."

"I'll tell Dad as soon as he comes in. Although, he'll probably want to let the sheriff talk to the fellow, he ought to know what's going on. I guess we should beat it right on out there." Louie didn't like the idea of his mother and baby brother out there alone in the house any more than Charlie. Even though C.L had a ranch hand, Bernie, and his wife, Agnus, and the two brothers felt better having their dad there, too.

"I'll hurry Avelle." Charlie hollered through the screen door. "Hey, Princess! Are you about ready?"

"Yes, hon. Just a few more things and you can take these suitcases into the car." Avelle whirled around the house like a tornado that touches down on the earth indiscriminately.

"Louie, if she starts to go riding before the sheriff gets out there, don't let her ride down by the river." Charlie spoke in a lower voice.

"Sure." Louie wondered how in the world he was going to keep Avelle from riding without letting her know what was happening.

"I don't want her to know, at least not until the Sheriff leaves, if he ever gets there. If she does, then she'll always be looking for somebody hanging around."

"Is that bad? I mean, shouldn't it be a good thing if she

kept her eyes open?" Louie puzzled at Charlie for wanting to keep his wife in the dark.

"Matter of opinion. Just because you know there's rattlers around doesn't mean you go looking for them. The way I see it, a person is safer if they don't go looking for trouble."

"Point there." Louie wasn't convinced. Avelle set the suitcases by the door and the two brothers put the luggage in the trunk of the Mercury. Charlie embraced his wife, folding her deep into his heart. For a moment Charlie thought about changing his mind. It was not only about them being apart tonight, but the job that would force upon them more nights of sleeping far from each other.

Louie pulled onto the highway and Avelle fixed her eyes on the river. She didn't want her heart to heal and desperately searched for a way to dam up her soul. Her search was futile. Avelle could no more stop the circle of life anymore than she could stop the circle of nature, for the stars that played a silent serenade upon the mighty Snake River would soon give way to the sunrise. So, too, her heart must heal and she must live the path laid before her.

Forrey was gone. Soon her Papa, Aunt Nell, and her brothers and sisters would move to Mountain Home. The time had also come for her little family to find their place to call home, and Charlie must begin his career as an Engineer.

Avelle bit her lower lip as her heart shouted a prayer to heaven. "How, dear God? How can I endure and accept all this change laid at my feet? Why did you let Forrey be taken from us? How could you let his life be cut short like this!?"

Louie was about to ask about Mountain Home when he saw Avelle wipe the tears from her eyes. Not knowing what to say, Louie held back his tongue and stared straight at the road, like when a deer stands mesmerized in the road, frozen by uncertainty of the oncoming vehicle's path.

Louie turned off the highway to the Brehan's ranch and stopped to look for any sound of an oncoming train.

"I've always hated this part. I feel like we are never going to cross the tracks in time before a train comes." Avelle confessed.

"Yeah, I know what you mean. Once when I was taking some livestock to market, I was crossing the middle of the tracks when I heard a train coming. I was sure as my shorts were messed that the train would do the slaughterhouses' job that day." Louie laughed at his memory.

# CHAPTER 21

THE BREHAN RANCH CONSISTED of twenty-three acres nestled between the Railroad tracks and the Snake River, eighty-eight acres across the highway extending toward the mountain ridge, and another 100 acres on top of the ridge. By a stroke of good fortune, C.L was able to acquire the homestead of his grandfather. Sean Brehan had come out from Colorado with the Railroad after losing the family mill in a high stakes poker game. C.L.'s father, Charles, was only ten years old when Sean Brehan died. Apparently, Sean Brehan had a heart attack while clearing the "petrified watermelons" off the eighty-eight acres in order to plant a crop of cantaloupes, watermelon, and honey dew. C.L bought the extra 100 acres on the ridge, once the ranch was his. The soil there was less difficult to clear and more conducive to growing watermelons.

It was an emotional day when C.L bought the ranch, because his father, Charles Brehan, had always dreamed of buying back the ranch his father, Sean, homesteaded but unfortunately also died an early death. Once the opportunity came, C.L felt it his legacy to buy back the ranch that was once lost.

The Railroad life must not have been far from Sean Brehan's heart because he built his homestead out of the lava rock on the ranch not more than 500 feet from the tracks. The almost 2,000 square foot two-story farmhouse was then built by the new owners. They, too, had 'train blood,' for the home lay only fifty feet further away from the tracks and less than a thousand feet to the east of the rock homestead.

Two Mulberry trees shaded the house on the east side, as well as one between the river and the old rock homestead. To the east, the land bent with the river as it edged its shore to the tracks. To the west, the twenty plus acres broadened wide and bordered the Colley Farm with their 100 head of sheep.

To the Brehan grandchildren, it was a place to hunt sand snakes and swing on the tire swing. The ranch served as a place to fish or skip rocks upon the glassy surface of the river. It was a place where they could gather the eggs from the hen house, milk a cow, feed and ride the horses, and plow a field without any of it ever being a chore.

The drive that brought Louie over the tracks was now parallel for 300 feet before coming to the open gate. It was no surprise to Louie that the gate was open. He hadn't shut it when he left earlier that evening. Yet to the amazement of both Louie and Avelle, C.L.'s 1946 Ford black pickup was parked in its usual spot...in front of the Mulberry tree closest to the fence where the tire swing hung.

"Looks like Dad's finally home." Louie parked his car where the headlights shined directly into the dining room where the light was already on.

"Looks like they're all still up, too." Avelle spoke with a relief that they wouldn't have to be careful not to wake anyone. It wouldn't have mattered any if they were asleep because just as Louie put his Mercury into park, he blared his horn scaring Avelle and startling the sleeping children.

It was Louie's intention to bring his father out the dining room door to help unload the children and the suitcases. He was not disappointed. The door hastily opened as Avelle and Louie stepped out of the Mercury. C.L.'s silhouette stood frozen for a moment between the yellow light of the dining room and kitchen and Louie's headlights.

"You mind killing the lights, son? You're making me half blind!"

"I got Avelle with me, Dad. Would you come help with the luggage and kiddos?" Louie turned off his headlights then went to open the trunk to remove the two suitcases. Nancy Ann stirred very little from her slumber in the front seat as Avelle cradled her youngest child. Chuckie whimpered to be carried and fell to his hands and knees when C.L tried to help his grandson out of the car. Kath protested that it didn't matter if she was the oldest. She needed to be carried, too! Cheerfully, Louie swooped his niece into his arms. C.L lead the way with Chuckie in one arm and a suitcase in his hand, as Louie and Avelle followed in a single file into the house.

"Crack some more eggs, Ernie. We've got company." C.L ordered his son as he led the way out of the kitchen and to the upstairs bedrooms.

"You mean we still have to cook now that Avelle is here?" Ernie's eyes grew to the same size, as the eggs he was holding, astonished that he would still have to choke down his father's cooking. Louie snickered, but Avelle sought to soften Ernie's anxiety.

"I'll be down in a minute. If you beat the eggs, I'll cook them up." Ernie relaxed as if the cavalry had just come charging to his aid at the very moment his life was in jeopardy.

Upstairs, C.L tucked Chuckie into Ernie's bed, and Louie brought Kath into Lisbeth's room where he had also set up the portable crib for Nancy Ann. C.L and Louie headed back downstairs while Avelle checked on Gladys.

"How are you feeling, Mom? Is there anything I can get for you?"

"Oh, Avelle! You're such a dear for coming out. With Agnus gone to be with her mother, I just didn't know what else to do."

Gladys sat upright in her bed wearing a rose-print duster. The covers were pulled back concealing the pink and red rosette patchwork quilt. Four pillows propped up her well-bandaged knee and ankle. Upon her lap lay an opened copy of *Pride and Prejudice by Jane Austin*. Avelle mused how her mother-in-law would still read a book that she could quote easier than scripture. Gladys had even named her only daughter after the spirited heroine, Elizabeth Bennett.

"Well, you cooked breakfast for us. The least I can do is come out and help you. I better get downstairs before the guys start cooking themselves. Would you like me to bring you up a tray?"

"No, just some coffee. C.L made me some toast earlier. I don't have much of an appetite."

Avelle left Gladys to her solitude. At the middle of the stairs she could hear Louie's desperation and the need for her to take control of the kitchen.

"Dad! The bacon's burning! Dear John! Where's the potholder?"

"Oh, sorry. Here you go."

Avelle stepped into the kitchen as Ernie pulled the potholder from his back pocket.

"Some place for a pot holder, I must say. That certainly can't be the only pot holder in the kitchen." Avelle took the potholder from Ernie and stepped in front of the stove, taking over the poor attempt at cooking.

"Nothing like the smell of burnt bacon to wake up an appetite, I'd say." Avelle choked and teased while waving her hand in front of her face like a windshield wiper on a stormy night. C.L and Louie proceeded to open the doors and windows to keep the burnt cloud from being trapped in the kitchen.

C.L and his two sons watched Avelle morph into an

octopus. The barely eatable charred bacon was transferred onto a plate. The breakfast potatoes were removed to an unused cool burner. Bacon grease ashes were wiped out of the pan with new butter placed in it to be prepared for cooking scrambled eggs.

"What I want to know is...where's Charlie?" C.L wanted the explanation of why Charlie had his brother bring his wife and family out to the ranch.

"I was meaning to ask you what this Mountain Home business was all about, Sis?" Louie piped in.

"Mountain Home? Why are you asking about Mountain Home?" C.L looked to Louie with confusion.

"Charlie stayed back at home because he was planning to go to Mountain Home with Nell in the morning. Why, I don't have any idea." Louie tried to explain what he knew to his father. Avelle turned from the stove with the coffee pot in hand and faced the inquisitive looks of her father-in-law and two brothers-in-law.

"I thought he had told you, Louie. Aunt Nell wanted him to take her. She's got an idea on how to use the insurance money." Avelle placed the coffee pot on the table and turned back to the stove, mostly because she wanted to hide her uncertainty of Aunt Nell's plan, and partly because the eggs needed to be put in the pan to cook.

"Forrey's money?" The tow broke out in unison, as well as shared perplexed looks and disapproval.

"There's nothing I could say that would begin to tell you how I feel about it. Maybe it would be better if I just skip it." Louie got up to serve the coffee and set the table, hoping that making him useful for the moment would help him keep quiet.

"What's her idea, Avelle?" C.L trusted in the thriftiness of Nell O'Brien, and if Nell had an idea, it would surely be worth hearing it out.

"Well..." Avelle sighed with hesitancy, unsure how she really felt about the rooming house idea. "Seems like she had this idea, that she would like to run a rooming house and...well...there is one for sale in Mountain Home."

"That's interesting. With all the children she has had to raise, you could almost say her whole life has been prepared for this very thing. Which one is it?" C.L's confidence in her step-mother gave Avelle the reassurance to support Aunt Nell.

"Someone named Steinmetz owns it."

"Steinmetz...Steinmetz...I don't remember that name." C.L paused for a moment then snapped his finger in the air as if the confession of not knowing someone had turned on the light bulb of memory in his mind. "Say, I bet that's the old couple who's running a rooming house out of that Victorian mansion. Yeah. I heard they wanted to sell. I bet she can get it for a good price, too."

"I hope so. Aunt Nell said that Mr. Steinmetz has arthritis really bad and that they wanted to move to Arizona. I hope they want to go bad enough to settle right away, and for a price Aunt Nell can afford." Avelle put the breakfast potatoes, scrambled eggs, and half charred bacon on the table, and laughed to herself because many times she had witnessed her in-laws eat breakfast at supper time.

"Sounds like a good deal after all," Louie chimed in. "By darn, it sure will seem pretty dreary around this little burg if the O'Brien's leave."

All mournfully agreed as C.L lead them in saying grace.

"Avelle, you sure do make this bachelor think twice about settling down." Louie remarked as he devoured his dinner.

"You know, Louie, yesterday a very pretty blonde brought me some letters Forrey had written her. She's living with her aunt in town. I'll bet you two would hit it off." Avelle smiled and winked at her brother-in-law.

"Playing matchmaker again are we? Well, I guess I might be ready this time."

"Oh, mercy! I forgot to get Mom her coffee!" Avelle jumped up from the table and with coffee in hand, headed back upstairs. She could tell once she had reached the top of the stairs that Gladys had already fallen asleep. Thinking it best to not wake her mother-in-law, Avelle turned back downstairs and almost ran into a very sleepy Ernie.

After good night kisses, Ernie went to bed and Avelle went back to the kitchen. Seeing the state of the kitchen, she mused to herself, "well, at least they scraped off the dishes and put them in a pile for me."

Not knowing where C.L and Louie went off to, Avelle set herself to work cleaning up as she would have at home unwilling to leave the night's job over until the morning. Then finally laying down on Charlie's old bed she cried herself to sleep again with tears that swelled and trickled.

# CHAPTER 22

THE WALK FROM THE house to the barn in the warm June night was not the conversation of father and son but rather the conversations of colleagues. The discussion dwelt upon opinions about the state of the world and the sacrifice their government asks of young men. They're asked to not only protect the freedom within their own countries borders but also to fight for the freedom of other countries.

The two men discussed the debated rights and wrongs of war, whether it is necessary or justified. They discussed the cause of the ideals and beliefs of nations and the effects on its citizens. The convictions held by a free people and their individual responsibility in life and the need to protect their nation and property.

As the conversation turned to the latter, Louie embarked

on relaying Charlie's sensitive message. A telephone had been installed in the barn for the primary purpose of calling the veterinarian. Without any need for concern of alarming the sleeping family in the house, C.L spoke earnestly into the mouth piece. Deputy Barett listened and agreed that dawn was the best time. Yes, he would be there early. Yes, they would bring a sufficient number of men. Everyone would be armed. A dangerous criminal was reportedly seen. He would certainly make every precautionary arrangement against the man's escaping, once caught. He knew who to notify, and would do so immediately. Yes, he would be grateful for the cooperation of the men who knew intimately the terrain. After the conversation broke C.L wiped the sweat from his brow.

C.L considered his personal posse while looking at his grown son but only asked a partial, well-understood question.

"Barney? I don't know, Son. What do you think?"

"I'd stake my life on him. It wouldn't be right not to have him along."

"Glad you feel that way."

The little house where Barney and Agnus called home was a refurbished smoke house that had been abandoned fifteen years earlier. It stood less than twenty-five feet from the ranch house's North end backdoor. Plywood had been laid over the sparsely spaced floorboard where the smoke would rise from fire below to cook the various meats hanging on exposed rafters. C.L closed in the roof and put an old caboose wood stove in the center of the single room building to utilize the existing chimney. A horse trough was also brought in for the comfort of a private bath.

Standing in the corner of the front porch, Barney greeted his unexpected guests with a deep contented voice. It was almost prophetic how his silhouette was hidden in the dark night and only the fire from his cigarette exposed his existence. Louie skipped a moon silvered pebble as Barney smirked with an exhale on how foppish the barely grown Brehan looked.

"Little quiet around here. Care for a little excitement?" Louie was almost giddy with the prospect of a grown-up game of cops and robbers.

"Cards, wine, or women?" Barney answered intrigued.

"Shoot 'em up cowboy."

"Me no got horse, Lone Ranger."

"Got swimsuit? Maybe go for little swim?"

"Got lead in pants. Where is it gonna be?"

"The cave by the river." Louie threw his head downstream.

"You mean the cave? The river right here?" Barney flashed an anxious glance at his boss, who nodded and finished out the conversation.

"Yep. He's right in the boy's little cave. Charlie saw him from dead-horse curve."

"When?"

"Friday. He saw him while 'gandy dancing' and Forbes saw him yesterday afternoon."

"Sheriff be out?"

"Yep."

"Day-break?"

"Yep."

"Guess I better get to bed then. Glad Agnus ain't home. Might have some explaining to do."

"Her mother any better?" Louie asked.

"I ain't heard. I was just thinking standing here, that I probably better get a letter tomorrow if her mother is better, and a phone call if she's worse. She'd have to be pretty bad for Agnus to call today, being Sunday and all."

C.L began to turn away and head in the house. "Yeah. Well, we'll holler then. I think Sheriff Frost will call me, but he might drive out instead."

"I'll be ready boss."

All three men went to bed with an ear cocked for the alarm.

At four o'clock in the morning Sheriff Frost called asking for their cooperation and the need to have them temporarily deputized for the search and capture of whomever it was. C.L decided to cut Sheriff Frost a little slack for not only his pompous attitude of mentioning the aid of the F.B.I but also dismissing the alert given by the very man to whom he was talking. Sheriff Frost had moved from Nampa to Mountain Home ten years ago and had won the recent election by a slim margin.

C.L woke Louie then made a pot of coffee while Louie got dressed and stepped out to get Barney. The coffee was scalding hot when Barney walked into the kitchen. It was obvious that Barney must have washed in the river because water was dripping from his graying brown hair like a dog who just took a swim and shook himself dry. They hadn't finished the first cup of coffee when car lights flickered from the turn after crossing the Railroad tracks. Sheriff Frost's headlights stopped at the gate announcing his arrival, which seemed to have impressed Barney because he was the first one out of the house.

"Holy smoke! Three cars!" He ran to the gate to let the police cars through as C.L and Louie waited in the drive.

Louie watched the men tumble out of the cars with amusement. Sheriff Frost was a stark contrast of his father who wore a solid blue-buttoned shirt, wrangler jeans, and round belt buckle and who was still as trim and fit as his father was in high school. The only hint of C.L.'s age was the grizzle at the temple below his thick dark hair with red undertones. Louie could have counted a full dozen men if he was able to count Sheriff Frost twice. Barney was standing again by his boss and his boss's son, all with rifles at their side and draped over their forearms.

"You Mr. Brehan?" Briskly asked Sheriff Frost.

"Yes, sir."

"Well, uh, as Deputy Barett informed you over the phone regarding this fellow on your property, we've got him for trespassing right off the jump. You say you know the terrain?"

"I've had this place for twenty years." C.L began feeling extra heat in his neck and his convictions reminded him of his personal respect for authority.

"Well, yes. I see. Now I don't want to alarm you, but we have to pick this fellow up, since he may be dangerous or even a subversive. If so, he may resist strongly. Unless you know how to use that firearm I'd advise you to stay here, we can manage."

Sheriff Frost almost took what he said back when he saw C.L calmly but strongly answer him with only a stare. C.L wanted to laugh at the absurdity of what Sheriff Frost insinuated. How could the sheriff know that C.L had survived the shores of Normandy with nothing but a few scratches? Sheriff Frost had yet to hear of how even the roughest, toughest bull would submit to the authoritative commands of its master, if given the proper respect.

Louie, however, was unable to hold the bristle forming in his mouth. He may yet prove himself in battle when his number came up, but he knew the rifle just the same.

"I've got my deer every year since I was ten, and two elk and a bear besides. I can handle a gun."

Deputy Barett walked up beside Sheriff Frost. "I know Mr. Brehan personally, chief. You would not have asked such a question if you had grown up around here. I will vouch for him without hesitation and I know he can handle these guns. If he says his boy and this fellow can shoot, you can count on it."

"Thanks Deputy Barett. I mean no disrespect, Mr. Brehan, with what we might be facing, I just needed to be sure."

Side by side, C.L and Sheriff Frost lead the party around the fence and west down the incline and across the flat. By the way C.L and Sheriff Frost spoke now to each other you would have thought C.L was giving a guided tour. With pride in his home, C.L gave intricate details of the ranch and life along the Snake River, sweeping his arm around on the land as if playing a violin. The official mowing group of men marched across the flat in the beginning light of the new day. In a few minutes they came to the spot where the land fell away to the river. Here the ground was studded with up thrusts of rock where a few scattered stalks of sage and bronco grass was the only vegetation. Sheriff Frost held up a hand signaling the men to stop.

"Now, men, it'll be full light in a few minutes. Here is what I want you to do." Sheriff Frost spoke in hushed tones and the men filed in a huddle receiving the instructions for their play.

Sheriff Frost divided the men into three groups. One, he directed to approach the cave from the west, and the second from the east. The third group was to stay above and watch with their rifles on the ready. Louie went with Sheriff Frost in the west group while C.L and Barney went to the east.

The Sun woke the sky with its full morning light. The birds sang their morning melody. The Snake River vociferously clapped upon its rocky bars, as if nature itself kept the hidden trespasser in a lulled sleep as his captors inched stealthily to surround the cave.

Barney was almost certain this plan would end in disaster as the east moving group struggled the steep bank clothed with underbrush of the same heavy sage and chokecherry bushes. A natural defile aided the men going west with the track that Louie and his brothers would often use. The tracks lead to the edge of the river where the water for the stock was hauled. Here the path ended at a curving sandy beach that leads into the cave.

As Sheriff Frost reached the sand with his men, he lifted up his hand with the silent command to stop. All the men seemed to take their eyes off the cave and its possibly dangerous fugitive and pondered the spot. It seemed the perfect spot for a private fishing hole or a lover's picnic.

Louie looked out across the river as the surface shined like a green glass betraying anyone who dare take the temptation of swimming between its lava rock shores. Many an animal and human being had been swept to their death by the hidden and deadly undercurrents. The orchard farm on the opposite shore gave a picture of a beautiful dream or an exquisite painting crafted by the most skilled painter.

On this most beautiful time of day with the clear promises of a new beginning, a throb of pity for the man in the cave rushed over Louie. Performing a very bad ballet recital, Sheriff Frost led his group with his rifle ready. As Sheriffs Frost cocked his firearm the nasty snick sound broke the peaceful morning.

"What a way for a man's day to start," thought Louie, "with rifles jammed down your throat." Louie looked up as he saw his dad and the other men that came from the east. "Boy they sure were quiet. I never heard a sound."

As if Sheriff Frost had given a signal by cocking his own rifle, the rest of the firearms cocked with a snicker in reply. Strange that the rattling of rifles and pistols that had warned the song birds away had not brought a stir to the cave.

"If the fellow was gone, we're all going to feel a little foolish for tromping out here like this." Louie again spoke to himself silently as he watched Sheriff Frost with a front row seat.

Sheriff Frost stooped down and went in, all rifles were ready aimed for fire at any moment. Louie and the men on the sand could now see what the sheriff saw, a lumpy figure in a khaki sleeping bag. Just as Sheriff Frost began to lean down and shake the trespasser, the fellow's dark eyes flew open in surprise. Looking at the men in astonishment, he sat up, slowly raising his hands.

The stranger appeared to be in his late forties, about the same size as the Brehan men but a bit more muscular. Louie noticed that his hands were work-worn, calloused, and continued to feel sorry that Louie's family had anything to do with depriving him of his liberty. "We should have at least offered him a bed and a meal." Louie scolded himself while a lock of the man's dark, fine hair fell into his eyes. The man made a motion to brush it back but thought the better of it.

"Come on out of there, sir, but watch those hands," Sheriff Frost barked. One of the deputies on the sand bar kept his rifle raised at the man's face while Sheriff Frost stooped and patted around the head of the bag.

"I ain't got no gun. Don't shoot, damn it!" His voice was surprised with a touch of a whiskey baritone. He wore a white sleeveless undershirt and astonishing red and blue plaid shorts. Some of the men snickered all the while grateful that the fellow did not sleep with less.

Louie noticed an alcoholic aura from the man when he spoke. Was he still a good guy, or maybe just a bum? "Still," Louie thought, "he kept a clean camp. The sack of food and a half full bottle of cheap whiskey lay beside neatly folded blue jeans and a blue chambray shirt resting on a small rock. Clean white work socks lay across the top of the work-worn boots.

The man reached out for his shirt as he watched the guns warily, only to get his hand slapped away by Sheriff Frost. After pressing the clothes for a gun, and looking a little ashamed, Sheriff Frost handed him his shirt. After turning over the boots in a continued search, he handed them to their owner as well. The man now dared to brush back his hair and yawn and stretch.

"Okay if I wash?"

"You can wash when we get you to town?" Sheriff Frost barked again.

"Aw, let him, Bill." One of the deputies pleaded.

"Let's just see who you are first." Sheriff Frost was in no mood to assume this fellow was just a simple bum or an innocent camper.

Sheriff Frost went through the sack of food again and found a worn brown leather wallet. The men generously fell back a little and lowered their firearms to let the fellow get dressed. As Sheriff Frost examined the contents of the wallet his face began to pale. He was holding a newspaper column and the man's drivers license. The cut of the headline read,

**"KILLER STILL AT LARGE."**

"He's Jack Sonerburg, boys!" Before Sheriff Frost's alert was finished, every rifle was jerked back to attention with every barrel angrily staring down on the fugitive. The week before he had robbed and killed a service station attendant-owner, his wife and daughter, and another man who happened to be in the isolated station along the Wyoming-Idaho border. Police in ten states were on the lookout and his capture would certainly do Sheriff Bill Frost's reputation no harm.

Arrogantly Jack finished getting dressed, combed his hair then put the comb in his front shirt pocket.

"Must say, you guys weren't takin' no chances. Did you call out the F.B.I, too? Thanks. I didn't realize how tough I was, I guess." Jack's laugh made a sick reaction in the men who guarded him. Though they all had respect for the law, it went without saying that they wished the trial and execution could happen right here on this spot.

"What did you do with the gun?" Sheriff Frost commanded.

"What gun? I ain't got no gun?" Jack smugly shrugged his shoulders as if innocent and casually placed his hands in his pockets.

"Listen Sonderburg, we don't have to play games with you. You boys pick up his gear and keep an eye out for the gun. C'mon, let's get out of here. Don't let him out of your sights for a minute. If he even looks like he will run, then shoot him."

Jack Sonderburg led his captures back up the track with Sheriff Frost and his rifle right behind him. The group of men that watched from above kept their gun sites on the fugitive until the men at the east of the cave could get caught up with Sheriff Frost. They met the men at the top at the same time the men charged with the duty of cleaning up and searching for the gun caught up with Sheriff Frost.

"No gun, Chief." One of the men reported.

"I picked a hideout right in somebody's back yard!" Jack swore in disgust and self-rebuke.

"How you made it this far, I can't figure out," commented one of the men.

"Left your car in Pocatello, didn't you Sonderburg," charged Sheriff Frost.

"I thought they'd find it right away. I was crazy to start out in it. I knew you all'd be looking for me between here and the coast," claimed Jack smartly as though he knew the mind of the police force that was hunting for him.

"How'd you get out of Pocatello?" Another officer asked more out of curiosity than for interrogation purposes.

"Hitch-hiked."

"Hitch-hiked? Boy, somebody must be nuts." Louie started to re-evaluate all the times he himself picked up hitchhikers.

"Naw, kind of nice old duck. Got a farm in Hagerman Valley. I crossed over the river there and walked on down." Louie gave a concerned look to his father and Barney wondering if the fellow meant old Ike Youree.

As the men continued their trek to the house and vehicles, the men couldn't help but be amazed with the fugitive who had come down on foot, not only just passing on the lava-rim rocks, or the river that was visible but unavailable for drinking water. There was also the rattlesnakes under every sagebrush and coyotes that made each night hideous. Whenever a rattlesnake chose to strike, the coyotes were sure to feast. The bleached bones might only be found many years later, if ever at all. No one ever would dare make that trek without being armed and on horseback, or if one dared on foot, NEVER without a pistol. It must have been courage, stupidity, luck, or Providence that allowed this killer to be found here...unharmed.

"Where did you hide your gun, Sonderburg?" Sheriff Frost asked again gruffly. To apprehend the fugitive was good, but to have the murder weapon would have been the whipped cream and cherry on top of the sundae.

"Naw," sheepishly answered the killer. "I threw it out in a clump of sagebrush right after I left the station."

The light manner in which the killer freely answered the impromptu interrogation further soured C.L.'s stomach. Here was a man hiding out on his property that had not just killed a man, but worse...a woman and her child. As they neared the ranch house he would no longer allow the killer to lead the trek.

"I better walk ahead, sheriff, just in case the kids are up and come running out."

Louie looked at his watch and was amazed to find it was already 6:45 a.m. It seemed only half an hour ago they were drinking coffee while waiting for Sheriff Frost.

"I'll go, Dad. I've got to eat and get out of here." Louie handed Barney his rifle and ran to the house. C.L still pressed to the front to escort the welcomed posse and the unwanted fugitive off his land.

# CHAPTER 23

AVELLE WOKE TO THE ringing of the phone or maybe it was just in her dream. She finally came to her senses when it seemed no one was answering the call. She slid from the covers, slipped into her house shoes and robe and hastened downstairs. It was Agnus. Surprised by Avelle taking so long to answer the phone she only asked that she speak to Barney.

"Yes, Agnes. I'll go right out and get him." Avelle promised, and wondered if Agnes's mother was worse or regrettably had died sometime in the night. Avelle opened the kitchen door she came through last night and stopped in her shoes.

"What in the world?" Three parked police cars behind C.L.'s pickup and Louie's Mercury, there was not a man in sight. "Some guard dog you are, King. What did you do, boy, send all the men running without waking any of us up in the house?"

King, a black and white Border Collie, rose up, yawned, stretched, and fawned Avelle to be petted, then followed her to Barney's house. When no one answered the door, Avelle wondered if she would have to hunt the entire twenty-three acres while Agnus impatiently waited on the phone? Not knowing where else to start looking, Avelle made her way back to the house. She heard someone running up on the other side, and hurried herself around the yard.

"Louie? What's going on?" Avelle asked determined to have a straight answer.

"Hm, uh, hello, Sis. Nothing. Wait till I get my breath."

"Where's Barney? Where did all these police cars come from?" Avelle demanded.

"They're coming." Louie answered breathlessly and thumbed the rest of his explanation toward the flats near the old homestead as the approaching men appeared. "What do you want Barney for?"

"Agnus is on the phone." Avelle answered distractedly as she saw C.L and Barney lead a pack of police all with firearms except for one who had his hands raised to his head.

"Oh. Well, I'll go talk to her. Come back in with me." Louie tried nonchalantly to lead Avelle back inside the house.

"I'll just go get Barney." Avelle took a step toward the

men but Louie caught her arm with a secure but not excessively tight grip. Avelle jerked her arm free and gave Louie a fiery stare that could have melted wax faster than any fire known to man.

"If you come inside, I'll give you a short explanation to a long story. If you come inside and put on a pot of coffee for me, you might just hear all of it." Louie smirked and winked hoping it would intrigue his sister-in-law enough to go inside. She did, and fully intended to hear the entire story.

Once Avelle was inside, Louie hollered for Barney to come to the phone. Jack Sonderburg was handcuffed and put in the backseat between two strong officers. Just as secretly they had entered the ranch, they drove back past the gate and over the Railroad tracks to claim their prize of capturing the now famous killer. A couple short sentences in the report would be the only credit the Brehan family would get for their alarm and assistance in the fugitive's capture.

Avelle couldn't remember a morning when making breakfast was not hectic. This morning was no exception. Louie had to be at Reverse, fifteen miles away, at 8:00 a.m. to start his work week as an operator. Barney would ride into town with him, then go on to meet Agnus. Agnus's mother was sinking fast and was in fact dead when he arrived the next day. Gladys woke and called out which roused Chuckie, who tried to crawl over Ernie who complained loudly enough to wake the baby. The crying summoned Avelle upstairs, which startled Kath from deep slumber. Everybody was up and ready to face the day.

In the aftermath of Louie's tumultuous departure, and now that everyone was fully awake, the family gathered around the bed in the master bedroom. Grandma lifted the covers to invite her grandchildren to snuggle up closely while Grandpa told his story about the scary troll who lived in a cave. Avelle warned her children to stay away from Grandma's hurt leg. C.L related the happenings of the morning but had to threaten Ernie with expulsion if he didn't quiet down during the story-telling.

The grandchildren stayed entertained with their grandmother as Avelle went downstairs to prepare breakfast while C.L and Ernie headed to the barn for a long overdue milking of the cows. While cooking breakfast, Avelle began to take apart the separator and found its cleaning had been neglected. A horrible odor of rancid cream rose from the inside of the separator as Avelle took out the gears, strainer disk and separator bowl. It was clean and dried when C.L and Ernie walked back into the kitchen with fresh buckets of milk.

C.L looked around with appreciation for his daughter-in-law's efforts. Not only was breakfast on the table, but also the separator was cleaned and ready for the morning's milk. Avelle had taken Gladys her breakfast and was on her way back down with her children in time to see C.L and Ernie perform the intricate, but not complicated task of milk separation. Kath, Chuckie, and Nancy Ann sat at the kitchen table with focused attention upon their uncle and grandfather.

"Avelle, would you please run the sink about half full of hot water. We'll need to set the other two buckets in so they'll warm up a little, or at least not get any colder." Avelle was busy with her instructions while C.L explained about the buckets of milk.

A pleasant hum of the separator began to fill the room with its first batch. Ernie took a blue pottery pitcher from the cupboard and a clean matching cup. He handed his dad the dipping strainer who proceeded to dip whole milk from the separator bowl into the pitcher. C.L.'s strong, steady hands were careful not to let any warm milk fall. With tender care the man and boy made the fresh milk as the three children's mouths drooled with anticipation. All seemed right with the world as Avelle also watched in peaceful silence.

After the process was finished and the full pitcher of milk was placed on the table, C.L led in a prayer of thanksgiving and the once peaceful moment was again turned to eating, talking and laughing. After breakfast, Ernie took the buckets of skim milk to the pig pen and the two penned calves. C.L continued to sip his second cup of coffee while Avelle re-washed the separator.

He continued to give her the news of the farm. A calf wasn't doing too well. A lack of sufficient spring rain run off threatened the lower patch of alfalfa, (which being in sandy soil required more that its share). Then, with coffee finished, C.L kissed his grandchildren and left for the hard but wonderful work that occupied farmers in June with an eager Chuckie on his heels. "Just for the morning," Avelle had agreed.

Gladys insisted that the children's toys be brought to her room. She was tired of the bed and wanted something to do besides read. Avelle promised Kath to take her for a short ride in the evening if she helped her grandmother, and stayed with Nancy Ann. Avelle was talking with her mother-in-law about quilting and needlepoint when Ernie called from downstairs.

"Hey, Sis?"

"Yeah?"

"Dad wants to know if you want Goldie brought in?"

"Oh, I uh, I don't know." The menstrual period from her miscarriage was still unrelenting in giving Avelle's abdomen fits, but to miss going for a ride on Goldie? Surely the ride would help. If she went, that meant the woman she came to help would be left to tend two girls instead of being tended, too. Avelle bit her bottom lip and reasoned that it would be best to turn down the much-wanted distraction.

"Yes, Ernie. Bring the mare in," billowed the order from his mother. Avelle tried to protest but Gladys would hear nothing of it.

"Nancy Ann will go back down for a nap sooner or later and then I'll send Kath outside to play. You girls want to stay with your grandma, don't you?"

Avelle reasoned within herself that there was no way she was going to win the argument with her mother-in-law, especially since she wanted to go anyway. So Avelle picked up Gladys's breakfast tray and hurriedly finished her work. Before going back upstairs to change, she prepared a lunch for the men to eat if they came in before she returned. Then darting back upstairs, she changed into the faded levis and red-checkered blouse that she always left at the ranch. Avelle folded Forrey's letter she had found on her end table at home. It was underneath the letters from Gloria and she put it in her back pocket. Avelle knew it was time to read his last letter whether she really wanted to read it or not.

Avelle ran to the barn with a guilty hurriedness where Goldie waited switching her tail. Goldie fit her name. She was a beautiful Mustang with her coat, mane, and tail that gleamed the color of gold, a pure golden nugget. Her eyes were set apart with intelligence, and more importantly, Goldie knew it. Some horses are independent of their owners and fellow human workers. Some horses are sullen and mean either from design of birth or the harshness of man's hands. Some horses are like Goldie, gentle and beautiful. She acted like you were another, slightly different horse. Or maybe, she thought she was some queer sort of human. She knew she was an intelligent horse, smarter than most men and more loyal than any dog she had ever seen.

Avelle loved her sweet tempered mare, everyone did. No one could approach Goldie without touching her and speaking to her. Avelle ran her appreciative hands over her withers, patted her neck, and fingered her feathery ears. Goldie arched her neck and rubbed against Avelle's hand like a big cat. Every time, Avelle wondered if sometimes she could hear Goldie purr.

"You do better at getting your saddle on, than the children do getting dressed, Goldie," complimented Avelle, to which, Goldie nickered in agreement. Out of good form, Goldie always protested the blanket a little but would stand with a waiting air as Avelle brought the saddle. Whoever saddled and harnessed her always felt that Goldie wanted to join in a good run.

Avelle led Goldie to the corner post of the barn in order to mount. A painful strain shot through Avelle, "maybe I shouldn't ride today after all." Goldie nickered again and stomped her left front leg with ears pricked and eyes focused on the river.

"Okay, we'll go. Just remember to take it a little easy today. Okay?"

Goldie shook her head and promised as the walk became faster and settled into a gentle canter with Avelle letting the mare have her head. Just in time, Avelle thought to look at the upstairs bedroom window. Sure enough two cheerful faces and small hands frantically waved. She waved back as she passed and headed toward the western meadow.

Woman and horse were daughters of the west. For those whose birth lay along the Snake, no other river could compare to its untamable beauty in the untamed west. From its origin in Jackson Hole county it brawls and shoulders through Idaho until at long last it is tamed by the Columbia. Looping through the southern part of Idaho it cuts through sun scorched lava canyons and mountain valleys in one grand arc. It boasts of sage green in summer, steel blue in winter, and gives little of itself along the banks. The placid sight has claimed more than one foolhardy soul who dared to swim its currents, for the Snake has no aversion to blood.

Looking out across the soft sage water, the orchard on the other side, and the grim lava canyon, Avelle got down from her horse to stand in the June sun. The story of creation in Genesis swirled in her mind as she wondered if there was any purpose to the design of this unforgivable land with rugged beauty that is hidden in the sagebrush preparing for the changing seasons that defy logic and definition of "high desert" land.

A soft warm breeze carried a hint of the secret perfume of the sagebrush, and life was peaceful and still until Avelle looked down where she stood. She was at the precipice of the sand and a shivered fear played upon her spine as she saw the footprints. Avelle knew in her mind that a creature had sought refuge here and had been denied, but now it struck home.

Another sister was grieving today. Another father was coming to grips with the loss of his son, daughter and grandchild. Indignation rose within Avelle for the malicious soul who had spilt blood and sought to take refuge on their soil. She felt disgusted by the coward who hid from his villainous deed. How could God allow men time and time again to rape, pillage, and murder? What good was mercy, grace, or freedom if constantly mocked by malcontents? Where was the guarantee that the sacrifice her brother felt burdened to take would bring about freedom in another country and thereby become an ally?

Would her country's involvement bring about peace to another nation like it did with Europe and Japan? Would soldiers be blamed if freedom over communism and socialism were not achieved? Would the President, Senators, Congressmen, and Generals admit their true convictions and accept the responsibility of sending men into battle? Or would they turn the blame to someone else to ease their own consciences?

The only solid answer to her questions...capturing the fugitive to answer for his crimes was worth the danger her in-laws faced. Avelle was all at once grateful for Charlie's sharp eye, and the trainmen who watched the ranch as they clattered by. Though she felt sickened and fearful, she also felt protected and watched over.

Avelle led Goldie to an eye thrust rock and upon mounting turned from the sand and cave. She had not come to gape at the sight of so much activity; she had not come to argue with herself about the politics and convictions of war. She had come to clear her head and heart. She came to think about Forrey without crying uncontrollably. She came to accept the changes that would be happening in a matter of days. She came to pray, to really pray. She came to find how to pray and seek guidance.

Goldie must have known exactly where Avelle wanted to go. Without any effort of directing, they trotted back past the house to the eastern edge of the property where the Railroad trusses crossed the stream that fed the Snake. A memory began to creep upon Avelle about the last time Forrey had ridden with her this way. There wasn't much enjoyment in her ride today but she rode anyway. Goldie slowed to a walk as the path led between the fenced pasture and the river.

"Do you have that letter I wrote you?" Forrey's voice whispered to her heart.

Pulling Forrey's letter from her back pocket, Avelle began to read, trusting Goldie to know her own way.

*My dearest Sis,*

*Greetings from Korea. I hope that everyone is safe and healthy, and that you are not having to work too hard looking after your brood. Tell that brother-in-law of mine not to work too hard either, and remember to stop and enjoy life once in a while.*

*I need to tell you about something that happened to me before I was shipped over here. First, I met a girl. Her name is Gloria. She reminds me so much of you. Anyway, we have been writing off and on, and mainly I have been writing about you. I don't think I will do that anymore. It doesn't seem fair to a woman to be talking so much of someone else, sister or not. I hate to say it but you were right. I just haven't found the right girl. I'm not saying it's Gloria, but she has opened my heart to think it truly is possible to have what you and Charlie have.*

*Second, about two weeks before I left here, I went to church with a couple guys from the base. There was some big meeting and I just went along for something to do, I guess. The preacher was like nothing I had ever seen or heard. He spoke loud and soft, he spoke like he knew what he was talking about. Like he actually had coffee with God before he came to preach, or something.*

*When I was sitting there, it was as if we were sitting at a table and the guy was talking right to me. Sis, there was no weak-minded stuff here, the guy was right-on make no mistake. So I went forward at the altar-call and prayed for God to forgive me, and I accepted Christ as my Savior.*

*I can't imagine what you must be thinking right now, but please read a little more and give your best to listen to your old brother, okay?*

*Church was just something to do. We just went because it was either there or the bar. There is a peace in me now. I feel like I am really living not just existing. I want to see Heaven, to see Christ. Heaven and Hell are not just places to say anymore, to me they are real places. It's not a place to either drink beer with friends or sit in a cloud being bored.*

*This all probably sounds pretty funny to you , but I would rather live believing this than living like I was before. I have found that the God that we paid little lip service to really cares about me and my life. Do you know God like this? I hope you do. If you were over here knocking on death's door every day, would you be ready to die? Don't scoff sis, these questions are not meant to annoy you.*

*I want to give you two Bible verses. Please promise you will read them and then write to me as soon as you can. You can either tell me off or ask me anything.*

*1 John 1:9 He that hath the Son hath life; and he that hath not the Son of God hath not life.*

*Romans 10:19 That if thou shalt confess with thy mouth the Lord Jesus, and shalt believe in thine heart that God hath raised him from the dead, thou shalt be saved.*

*Your loving brother,*

*Forrey*

If Avelle hadn't felt her riding boots securely in the

stirrups she surely would have fallen right off her horse. She wasn't surprised that Forrey had gone to church, they all had, with the exception of Papa. There was little memory of going to church when Mama was alive, yet there was always a sense of trust in God. The only Bible in Avelle's possession belonged to her mother. It held the list of marriages, deaths, and births of strangers that were called family.

At first Aunt Nell would walk the children to church in King Hill, but stopped after the ice-house accident. Papa, to her knowledge, had never stepped inside the doors of a church with the exception of her wedding. Though he had no objection to any of his family going, he would always remind them when they returned, "No use talkin' to this old reprobate. Don't you go on 'bout that stuffy preacher's talk or them sanctimonious churchgoers. I got no use for them, 'cuz God got no use for me."

It was Forrey's absolute certainty of his belief in God, in Christ, that threw Avelle for a loop. How could he be so certain? Did the guys talk him into something? Was there some magic to kneeling at an altar? She had knelt at an altar. She had prayed. She believed in God and believed that Jesus died on the cross. What was different about Forrey that would cause him to write such a letter? Maybe he had some premonition that he would die in Korea and decided to ease his conscience.

Goldie stopped at the creek and dipped her head down to drink the cool spring run-off water. Across the highway to the northeast were the flat lands, which was a stark contradiction from the southwest. There on gentle rolling hills and distant tablelands grew a million shades of tawny green. Avelle got down from Goldie and patted the perspiration that signaled the warm morning and would soon become a hot June day. Avelle felt the temptation of taking a swim in the creek but decided to simply take off her boots and shoes to wade her feet.

Picking up Forrey's letter again her eyes fixed on a question he had asked. *Do you know God like this?* Why did that question bug her so much? It felt like a mosquito that buzzed around her ear that she couldn't swat away. *Don't scoff sis, these questions are not meant to annoy you.* She was annoyed, and yet some sort of pain began pleading from the inside. It wasn't her abdomen since that quit hurting a while ago. What if Forrey was right? Was he right? Words began to bubble from her mouth before she realized that she was actually praying, really praying.

A peace began to wash Avelle's soul as the water in the creek refreshed her feet. She began to cry. She cried not because of grief but because it felt like a burden had been lifted from her, like how Mustangs pinned in a tight corral race freely when the gate is opened upon an unfenced meadow. As sure as she knew her own name, now she knew the voice of God. He was the Shepherd, she was the lamb. Is this what Forrey felt and meant when he said that Heaven was now real to him? Her sorrow of Forrey's death was beginning to turn to joy. Somehow she knew she would see Forrey again. It was now not words to say, but the real true sap that heals the tree. Her tears of grief had turned to tears of joy. Now she would head back home, the same Avelle, but yet changed.

"Charlie isn't here yet?" Avelle asked Ernie when she brought Goldie back into the barn.

"Nope. Did you have a good ride?" Ernie began to take off Goldie's saddle and harness and brush her down before letting her out in the pasture.

"The best!" Avelle almost laughed and kissed Ernie on the forehead.

Ernie watched Avelle walk lightly to the house.

"What on earth got into her?" Ernie asked Goldie. Goldie just nickered, as if to laugh the secret to herself and raised and shook her head.

About two in the morning Charlie startled Avelle out of a deep sleep when he crept into bed beside her. She hadn't heard the car come in. She had held supper back a little still expecting him at any moment. Now he finally came in. Without turning on the light he had slipped out of his clothes and took her tightly in his arms. "Was he seriously amorous?" Avelle's accusation was pricked when he broke into sobs and wept until he was exhausted. Without a word passing between them, Avelle tenderly held him until he fell sound asleep, then laying there herself, pondering an explanation until she herself drifted back asleep.

# CHAPTER 24

IN THE MORNING EACH member of the family had much to tell. Words tumbled and fell from their lips as they laughed and interrupted each other. The two hours before Charlie left for work were crowded and jammed with news. That morning would be the beginning of the most hectic week Avelle would experience in all her life.

Yesterday morning Charlie just finished shaving when Clarence knocked on the door. Charlie stammered for a morning greeting at the surprise of his caller being his father-in-law and not one of his brother-in-laws.

"Relax, Charlie. I knew Nell'd have some sort of notion in her apron. I just wish we'd a come into it some other way." Charlie noticed the sobriety he had seen in Clarence yesterday still carried through till this morning.

"So...you're okay with this?" questioned Charlie.

"Sure. Nell's practically born for this. Least this way she'll get paid by those she's carin' for."

After breakfast, Charlie, Clarence and Nell traveled to Mountain Home. The only conversation for the twenty-mile journey was the abrasive protest of the Jalopy. After formal greetings were made, Charlie and the O'Briens found the owners quite anxious to sell the rooming house. The contract concluded over a single cup of coffee. Understanding that the O'Briens must wait for the insurance money to come through, the agreement was sealed with an undated note for full payment. Nell would wire the money as soon as it came in, and agreed to take the reigns within two days. It seemed that the owner's nephew and his bride were passing through from their honeymoon and returning to California. The new couple graciously consented to transport the elderly couple to their destination in Arizona. Charlie felt the whole deal was moving way too fast, yet grateful that Clarence was there to participate in the deal.

Once the arrangements were settled, the Stienmetzs gave the O'Briens and Charlie the grand tour of the newly acquired enterprise. The Stienmetzs were not blessed with children of their own and had been running rooming houses their entire forty-five years of marriage. Fifteen years ago the couple moved out to Mountain Home on a whim. Arthritis was just setting into Mr. Stienmetz's joints. They thought the dry climate of Idaho would be just the therapy he needed without having to give up the beauty in the changing of the seasons.

The rooming house sat on a corner lot near the highway turn-off that lead to the air force base. The Stienmetzs built this particular rooming house to look more like a home than the standard rectangular architecture. The inviting Victorian stick style home had three stories with a basement foundation and painted white with a red-shingled roof. The west-facing porch was decorated with swings on each end and chairs for the guests comfort.

The third story divided itself into two parts; an attic for storage and a honeymoon suite with its own private bath. Mrs. Stienmetz would often leave the suite unoccupied but would rent it out as a short-term apartment from time to time. The second floor held eight rooms and two bathrooms. One bathroom was designated to men and the other to women. The maximum occupancy for the rooming house could reach thirty-four residents; however, Mrs. Stienmetz kept the residents closer to around twenty.

The main floor held the large formal dining room, a library, the gathering room with davenports and card tables, the kitchen and breakfast nook. Behind the kitchen was the owner's two-room apartment with a private bathroom and access to the basement. In the basement were the furnace and laundry room, as well as plenty of space to board up walls for bedrooms for the O'Brien brood.

After the tour and lunch, the O'Briens were introduced to their grocery supplier then they headed back to King Hill. Charlie fired up the Jalopy while Clarence escorted Nell into the backseat as their emotions spun with the realization of business ownership.

"Would you like me to take the two of you back home? I need to go to the bank and hunt up Vogler."

"You gonna get the Plymouth?" Clarence asked, proud that he had a part in the deal.

"Has Avelle seen it?" Nell asked while pulling from her purse a white handkerchief with a crocheted daisy-lace border patting her neck and face dry.

"No. I don't want to layoff another day if I know we're going to get it anyway. Besides, I'm gonna need a better car to help you folks move, not to mention all the driving back and forth for visits we'll be doing." Charlie smirked a wink at Clarence.

Leaving Mountain Home, the highway followed the section of twin Railroad tracks commonly known to all Railroad employees and those who lived in those parts as 'Reverse.' Charlie watched the tracks and looked forward to the day he would officially be an Engineer.

Engineers and trainmen are not bound to the milepost limits like the section crews are, but their work orders are set by, 'sidings.' Every siding on the work order shows the yard limit of either the drop-off or pick-up or both for cargo ordered by the customer. Although the milepost limits that laid before them was monotonous, the sidings brought variations to the job. Would they pick up three cars or thirty cars, or would they drop off any cars? Which sidings would they go to? Which sidings would they pass? Would they be gone the usual sixteen hours or would they be sleeping overnight at some distant railroad terminal?

They worked outside and independently with the thrill of whom would make a better train and run it the most efficiently. The Engineer's job duty required him to stay in control of the entire train. The Conductor's job duty required him to piece together the cars of the train for that day's customers. The Engineer and his Fireman, the Conductor and his Brakeman passed the long hours with competitive banter as each man claimed the perfection of the train as his own birthright.

Forbes' lunch was once again interrupted by the expectedly unpredictable telephone call given all trainmen that they are to report to the yard within the hour.

"Who do I have with me?" Forbes always liked to know with whom he would be working.

"Starrett is your Fireman. Jones is your Conductor, and Finchman is your Brakeman." The Dispatcher answered back placidly, everyone always wanted to know with whom they were working.

"Well this should prove an entertaining run. See you in an hour." Forbes hung up the phone and headed once again to the hall closet to grab his grip. Everything was there: A change of clothes and his travel toiletries, his notebook where he recorded all the sightings for each work order, extra reports to be turned into the clerk for Dispatch, and the only thing missing was his thermos and his lunch pail.

"Claire, you got my coffee brewing and my food?" Forbes hollered out.

"Well what do you think, Cecil? I've only been doing

this for thirty years!" Claire spat back. Cecil was supposed to have talked to young Charlie Brehan about buying their home. Now she would have to wait for another three days before any arrangements could be made for Cecil's retirement, as well as their move east to be with their only daughter and her family.

Cecil ignored his wife's scornful glare as he walked out the door. Claire had been nagging him for the past five years to move east with their daughter. Now as the ticking clock of retirement wound down, both of them were more than a little anxious to begin their last stage of life. Almost every phone call gave Forbes his escape from the demands at home as he ran his train along the steady earth and under heaven's sky. Everyday was still exciting and new but just like the unpredictable Idaho weather, the Trainman could go from loving his job to wishing he had never chosen the profession. Today was that day for the three men who sat riding in the Engine and the Brakeman who sat back in the Caboose. Before the work order would finish, Forbes would be all too grateful to retire and move east.

"Looks like we got some boys tamping the ties up ahead." Charlie brought the attention of the riders to the scene on his left.

"Must've gotten a call for that freighter down yonder, cuz' they're all moving off, except that one," Clarence added.

Indeed the section crew they saw working on the rails had just received a radio call to expect Forbes' freighter.

They had left the Glenns Ferry yard a half hour ago and they should expect to see it approaching at any moment.

"What's that knot-head doing still standing on the rails?" Clarence put his eyes on the worker a little more than a half a mile away from them as Charlie stopped the car.

Charlie could see the rest of the section crew waving at the worker whom Clarence had brought to their attention. The crew had split off the tracks to either sides of the right-of-way but one crew member was resting his forearm and chin on a pick used for digging out damaged ties, without any notion of danger.

Forbes was approaching a mile when he saw the crew leave the tracks and began to blow his whistle to send the last worker off the tracks. The closer he came, the more determined his warning whistle blew. Aggravation filled every pore of Forbes's body, "Was this yahoo seriously ignoring his call to get off the tracks?"

"Maybe he thinks the train's coming on the other set of tracks?" Nell tried to reason calmly.

"The fool's gonna get himself killed and we're forced to helplessly watch!" Clarence cringed at the thought of the consequence of negligence and laziness.

The section crew, the train crew, and the bystanders, (Charlie, Clarence, Nell) all seemed to shout in unison.

"GET OFF THE TRACKS YOU IDIOT!" The worker waved off the warning as if annoyed that the picky "rule keepers" were interrupting his peaceful slumber. Company regulations stated that if a train was approaching the site

231

where they were working, the crew were to not only get off the tracks, but also move out 150 feet into the right-of-way.

Just before Forbes reached a quarter-mile, he aggressively slapped the brake handle into the emergency position. Air escaped the brake line through to the valve in the cab and breezed past Forbes ear as if steam was also escaping his brain for having to stop 900 tons of diesel engine, 150 freight cars, and a caboose. Stopping 8000 tons of train could not (even in one's best imagination) stop on a dime, especially for one idiot who should know better than to be standing in front of a train.

Twenty-six pounds of pressure left the cylinder collapsing the piston, forcing the brake to clinch the wheels as the sparks flew. It would be a good mile before the train would be stopped. Specialists could only remove from the scene whatever was left of the remains of anyone hit by a train. The dispatcher told Forbes to fire the train back up and finish the work order, that there was nothing they could do but stay on schedule.

Nell waited in the car as Charlie and Clarence walked across the golden grassy plain to meet up with Louie and the Section Crew. They spoke together with grief in hushed and aggravated tones, while waiting to give their witness to the Company Inspector.

The rest of the drive back home was sullen. Nell had indeed guessed correctly, the worker truly thought he was on the opposite track and that he would only get the draft of the passing freight train.

Just as a child is scolded for touching the delicate veins

of the monarch's wings, (for if they are broken, its freedom of flight is now paralyzed). The earth reprimands its human inhabitants of the disregard to the fleeting preciousness of life. It holds the spilled blood within its pores as a suckling babe is held in its mother's arms.

How will one utilize the sand within their own hour glass? Will they harden the grains together as if to somehow resist their journey? Will they disregard the lessons they see and pass through life unchanged? Will they smooth out the grains to change into a glass to better perceive, learn, walk, or grow with the time they have been given?

Charlie, Clarence, and Nell did not need the afternoon's warning to the vapor of life. Yet here they were driving back home staring into their own heart and soul for that meaning and the realities or assumptions of an eternity. Had it been Louie leisurely standing there on the tracks, their day and the morning's excitement would have been vanished by grief. Though as it was, they could only dwell upon the speculation of a stranger's mind. Today they would be the sympathizers of those now forced to grieve the newness of loss.

The stark reality of life would force these three witnesses to finish out their day. Charlie would get a new car as well as back into road service as a Fireman by next week. The Jalopy would be set aside to be used for transporting the O'Brien brood to Mountain Home and then sold. Clarence and Nell would begin organizing their household and prepare for the move.

After dropping off his in-laws, Charlie intended to drive

out to the ranch and show off the new Plymouth. First, however, he refused to meet back up with his family without a handful of candy.

"Evening Bix." Charlie greeted the store clerk.

"Evening Charlie. What brings you in here, licorice for the kiddos?"

"I'm heading out to the ranch tonight, so you better load me up with enough for the big kids, too." Charlie winked with amusement as Bix chuckled and filled the order.

Handing a full bag of licorice, gobstoppers, jellybeans, and malt balls, Bix remembered the message he was to give to Charlie. "Hey Charlie, there was a stranger in here just before you walked in. Said he was a friend of yours. I didn't know where you were, so I just sent him over to your place."

"Thanks Bix, I'll go right over." Charlie lifted his bag in a farewell salute and drove across the highway to his home.

Bud Afton was turning from the front door when Charlie pulled up. They had served together on Charlie's last tour. Laughingly they came together in a comrade's embrace. With arms around each other's shoulders, Charlie escorted his shipmate into the house for coffee.

"What are you doing clear out here, Bud?"

"I'm on my way to Mountain Home for a revival meeting this weekend."

"A revival meeting? Since when did you start going to church?" Bud had always scornfully teased Charlie for not joining the boys for beers when they were on leave. Charlie's nickname had been, 'Preacher Boy' or 'Chaplin' even though Charlie rarely spoke about his faith.

"Oh, about a year after I got out. I was down in California learning how to surf, carousing around, just making a general nuisance of myself. One evening there was a group of guys standing around passing out pamphlets with one guy hollering at everybody saying they were all going to hell. I ended up taking one and just stuffed it in my trousers."

The coffee pot finished percolating on the stove and Charlie got a couple of cups from the cupboard, amazed at what he was hearing.

"I started remembering the few times we had talked about God, and how you were considering becoming a Naval Chaplin and all. Well, I read that tract and it all just stuck in my crawl. You know what I mean?" Charlie just smiled and sat the coffee down on the table.

"Well, after a couple of days I just couldn't get it out of my head, so I knelt by my bed and prayed. When I got done praying, I packed my sea bag back up and went home to North Dakota. A couple years went by when I heard about a preacher down in Texas who had a school for men whom God had called to preach. Now I'm not saying, I wanted to be a preacher, I just thought it sounded like a good way to learn about the Bible. So I went down there, went to the school, started helping out with the church and the pastor, and here I am on my way to a revival meeting in Mountain Home."

Charlie couldn't help but enjoy the sparkle in Bud's eyes. Long into the night Bud spoke more about his experience.

Charlie brought Bud up to speed on his own life as well as the past week. Bud was determined to make it to Mountain Home no matter how late it was, but promised to come back to help his family move. As it turned out, Bud had made plans to stay at the very same rooming house Charlie's in-laws were planning to take over. With Bud back on the road, Charlie yearned to see Avelle and talk to her. With the candy still in the front seat, Charlie resumed his earlier plan and went off to the ranch.

# CHAPTER 25

THURSDAY MORNING WOULD BEGIN the new dawn in Charlie's career. A few more men had yet to retire before Charlie would graduate to Engineer, and although it would be another couple of years, today he became one step closer.

"Did you hear about this trip of Forbes?" George Potter sat at his desk where the blackboard filled the wall behind him listing out the work orders, trainmen, and the respective trains for everyone to see.

"Yeah, I was bringing the in-laws back from Mountain Home when we witnessed the accident." Charlie responded in a melancholy tone.

"That's only the half of it, Charlie!" exclaimed George Potter.

"What are you talking about, George?"

"When you saw him he was deadheading to LaGrande. Apparently on his way back, someone stalled on the crossing in Payette."

"You'll never guess who he hit, either." Johnson came walking out of his office to join the conversation.

"Who?" Charlie couldn't help but ask.

"Cranky old Gus."

"You're kidding! What was Gus doing in Payette?" Charlie would have put money down that Gus would still be terrorizing the town by the time Charlie retired.

"Dropping off his wife. She went to go visit a sister she has there," explained Johnson.

"Is he still out?" Charlie directed his question to George Potter.

"He should be pulling into the yard in about twenty minutes."

Earlier in the morning as C.L and Ernie set out to milk the cows and leaving Charlie another hour of undisturbed slumber, Avelle got up herself. She woke with a foreboding feeling that up until now their life had been lived in calm waters. In her heart she wanted to beg Charlie simply just to stay on the section crew. It certainly wouldn't be long before he could become the section foreman. They had a home and if Charlie became the section foreman, then it would be officially theirs, as far as the Company was concerned. It had been wonderful for Charlie to step out his back door and be at work. He was always home every evening and on the weekends.

"Life seems more complicated than the lives we read about in books," Gladys had mused to Avelle the other morning. "Boy and girl meet, they fall in love, he is independently wealthy, and she never has a care in the world. The book ends with the family together and everyone still in love."

Downstairs she took up C.I's Bible and began to look for encouragement. Every page looked like a garbled language she couldn't understand.

Turning to her knees, she closed the Bible and laid it on the seat of the davenport. Her heart softened as an inquisitive child needing reassurance that the journey set before her was safe. Avelle's hands clasped tightly together as if clutching to her Heavenly Father's hand as she took her first steps of faith.

"Heavenly Father, I know I should be kneeling, but I feel like I should be in Church to pray to you. I hope it's okay that I'm talking to you like this. I really don't know what else to do." Tepidly Avelle began her prayer, but soon felt like she was talking to a new friend that was ready to give her anything her heart would ask, "Keep Charlie safe and help me to be flexible with his irregular work schedule. The kids and me are not going to see him as much, so please help me to make the most of the time when he is home. Help me make it easy for him to come home after every trip and may he feel the warmth of the love of his family when he goes to work. Amen."

Avelle sat back down on the davenport and realized she

had been trying to read C.L.'s Bible in Leviticus and remembered Charlie telling her that the best place to start reading the Bible was in John and Romans. As she began reading in the book of John, peace refreshed her heart as the stress of life began melting like the snow melts on the mountains in spring.

Avelle cheerfully sent Charlie off to work that Thursday morning, and as Avelle finished washing the breakfast dishes at the ranch, she reminded herself of Charlie's dream. She had her dream as a wife and mother and now it was Charlie's turn to achieve his dream.

When relaying this story to her grandchildren, Avelle would say that God gave her the two most hectic weeks of her life to produce two important life skills. One, a sense of humor with sudden changes. Two, to enjoy every moment of life by not making it conform to her own expectations.

Charlie was called back into road service, and Aunt Nell was in Mountain Home with the oldest twin boys. Agnus with low spirits took the role of custodian on the ranch while Gladys continued to mend. Avelle took herself and the children back home, not only to pack her folk's belongings, but also prepare her own family to become the new owners of the Forbes' home.

That Saturday morning most every car, truck and trailer available for use of the King Hill residents was packed up with the remaining possessions of the O'Brien brood. Avelle made sure every box had some sort of a label, (plates, bowls, silverware, cooking utensils, clothes sorted only by size and sex), to the point where it took longer for Avelle to pack the items than it did for the men to load and unload all the boxes and furniture.

"Sure is gonna feel like a lonely place with them out of the neighborhood." Louie Brehan mused to Bud Afton as the two stacked the last of the furniture into C.L.'s truck.

Aunt Nell showed Avelle all around the rooming house while directing where boxes and furniture were to be placed. Connie and Maggie were set to the unsuccessful task of keeping the smaller children out of the way when Nora suggested the girls start games of London Bridges, Red Rover, and Duck-duck-goose. It was well after lunch time when all the vehicles were emptied back out and everyone started looking like a pack of starved dogs.

"I'll have sandwiches made before you start digging a pit to roast one of those stray cats you saw." Aunt Nell laughed at the men who began to perk up at the mention of food.

With everyone finally settled with sandwiches, the same Thunderbird that Avelle had seen picking up Dora last week, pulled up to the rooming house's parking lot.

"Where's *she* been?" Avelle inquired.

"I haven't seen her since last night when the two of them took off," Aunt Nell confessed with a dropped head. "I suppose I should've worried, but I was just too tired. I kind of forgot she wasn't helping unload over here."

"He seems like a strong enough chap. An extra pair of hands would have come in handy today," Louie piped between bites of his sandwich.

"Looks like we get to meet this one, she's walking in with him," Clarence curiously noted. Never before had anyone seen the beau that would pull up to their home, and now the two came waltzing in, glowing in smiles of fresh love like a rose bud just opening its petals in spring. Dora wore a new pink cotton sundress with new white Mary Jane shoes and matching pink gloves, purse and hat with a mesh over her eyes. Her beau walked in dressed in his Air Force dress uniform holding his cover in his hands.

"Folks, I'd like you to meet Lt. Gary Halverson," she announced. Nora smirked to herself that he didn't really look like Rock Hudson, more like a tall, skinny and awkward brother of Rock Hudson. Dora began making introductions and suddenly everyone was conscious of their own disheveled appearance.

"Well, I have an announcement to make. Gary and I were married last night in Elko." Dora chirped with no regard the surprise would have on her family, especially her parents.

As mouths gaped around the room with the shock removing all air from their lungs, Clarence piped his disapproval of Dora not even mentioning her intention to them last night.

"Are you pregnant?" Clarence gruffly accused.

"No Papa, I am not pregnant! I'm eighteen aren't I?! Gary and I love each other, and I wasn't about to have my wedding bloodied by Forrey's money!" Dora clinched her fist that looped in her new husband's arm.

"Dora, you're Father is just saying that it 'a been better if you would have at least let us know ahead of time." Aunt Nell tried to plead reason into her eldest daughter.

"Oh, Mama. It's not like you'll be losing me right away. I'll still come over and help with the rooming house, that is until Gary gets reassigned to another base." Dora confidently declared. "Oh, Mama. Aren't you happy for me?" Dora begged with tears.

"Well, of course we are." Aunt Nell hugged her daughter and then hugged her new son-in-law. "Welcome to the family, Gary."

"Thank you, Ma'am." Gary's voice held a hint of Kentucky.

"I aint sure yet what kind of man you are Lieutenant, but we'll find out soon enough." Clarence eyed his new son-in-law like a hawk circling around his prey. "Preacher Afton here has invited us all to church in the morning, and by-gum we're all gonna find our best clothes and go to church as a family."

A feather mindlessly drifting through the kitchen could have knocked everyone down like dominos. It seemed that this day had been destined to be full of surprises. Timmy choked on his last bite. Charlie looked inquisitively at his father-in-law. Everyone had now noticed the new sobriety of Clarence O'Brien, but none would have suspected voluntarily going to church without it being a wedding or a funeral.

⌘

The O'Brien brood, along with their two son-in-laws, filled up two rows of the little country church in Mountain Home. All the while the congregation sang, most of the children kept looking around as if the roof would fall in on them, or they would be singled out as outcasts. Aunt Nell looked around nervously trying to smooth out her purple cotton dress.

The song leader stopped the congregation's singing and everyone turned around to shake hands with friends. Church members shook the hands of the large family who looked at those who welcomed them with fear of their very existence being judged. Yet, there was something in their smile and kind words of; "Good to have you here," and "Welcome," that contradicted the assumptions of sanctimonious churchgoers.

"Welcome everyone," began the Pastor. "I would like to introduce Bud Afton to all of you. For the last four years he has been working with Brother Douglas down in Texas and I asked him to come up this weekend to preach. Brother Afton, welcome to Mountain Home."

Bud Afton walked up the three steps to the platform and shook the Pastor's hand.

"Thank you, Pastor. This is truly an honor to speak to your congregation and visitors this morning." To everyone sitting in the auditorium Bud Afton looked calm, composed, and full of Divine unction, however inside his heart, fireworks were bursting louder and brighter than any known Fourth of July celebration.

"Would everyone please open your Bibles and turn to 2 Peter 3:9. As you are turning there I want to challenge your thoughts about who God is as well as who God is perceived to be by us as human beings." Bud Afton looked around the congregation. Some still fingered through their Bible. Some sat alertly and ready to listen. Some fidgeted with their clothes and hands and also their neighbor.

"I have not always been a Christian but I have always accepted the fact that there is a God somewhere. Before I got saved I assumed that some force beyond gravity held our world safely in space. I assumed that at times this force, this God only started what we all see and then has pretty much left us alone." Bud Afton looked at his notes again, then walked to the side of the pulpit and rested on his forearm as if getting ready to have a personal discussion with everyone seated.

"It seems to me, that most people who claim to be Christians unintentionally treat God like this. As if to say, 'Thank you for saving my soul, now leave me alone.' Or people who have had a rough time of life think of God, if they think of him at all, as some mad man playing chess. Maybe you're here today thinking that God is laughing at the demise of us here on earth, or that He must not be a loving God because he would rather squish people under his boot like ants rather than help them through their struggles." Bud Afton stomped his foot down on the ground imitating his words.

"Do you think God looks for decent people just to take his mighty baseball bat only to beat their lives senselessly? Then stand back and laugh sadistically at the bloody corpse laying on the ground and those kneeling around weeping." Bud Afton stopped for a moment, his eyes searched the congregation as he prayed in his heart, "Lord, please help me to show who You are and break any false pretenses they may have about you. Amen."

"Ladies and Gentlemen, who I described to you is not God but Satan!" Bud Afton lifted his finger to heaven then pointed his finger to the ground.

Still standing next to the pulpit, Bud Afton continued. "Have you ever seen a professional chess player? A year or so back a friend of mine had a brother who was to compete in a chess meet. We went to this huge auditorium where several dozen tables held chess sets and timers. Each time someone would move they would stop their time and the other would make their move then stop their time. I watched them all play until there were two men left. My friend's brother just happened to be one of them and ended up being the winner."

"I can play checkers, but to be honest, chess is a little out of my area of skill." Bud Afton smirked with laughter and the congregation joined him. "I talked with my friend's brother about what it takes to be a good chess player. He told me that a good chess player observes the entire board. He not only knows what moves he intends on making but anticipates the moves of his opponent. Each move is to be made with skill and precision. He must take great care to ensure that the outcome is to his advantage. He grieves over any piece he loses and is eager to snatch all of his opponent's pieces."

Bud Afton then returned behind the pulpit. He looked out at the congregation and saw that he seemed to have everyone's attention, but did he have the attention of their hearts and minds? More importantly, did the Holy Spirit have the attention of their hearts and minds? Bud Afton knew better than anyone that all the talking in the world would not make one budge of difference unless God was riding upon the air of the room speaking to each individual personally.

"Everyone please look at the passage I asked you to turn to earlier." Bud Afton cleared his throat and took a drink of water that had been hiding from the view of the congregation. "The Lord is not slack concerning his promise, as some men count slackness; but is longsuffering to us-ward, not willing that any should perish, but that all should come to repentance."

"Not one person can assume that God should or could keep our lives or the lives of our loved ones from trouble. We all must remember that from His vantage point He looks not only at the eye-to-eye contact that we see everyday but the entire movement of civilization. He perceives from eternity clear past through eternity future. He knows what moves Satan takes, and the choices we make in life."

Bud Afton picked up his opened Bible and walked around to the right of the podium. Towards the back row a mother bent down her head to instruct her child in some behavior and lifted her head back up again.

"Within the pages of this book you can find help for every decision you need to make in life. Within the pages of this book you can better understand yourself and you can better understand what God thinks of you, the world, or your neighbor. Within the pages of this book you will find how much God loves you and why He will or won't do something you think He should." Bud Afton walked back behind the podium as deep voices cried, "Amen" from the congregation.

If any in the O'Brien brood had not been fully paying attention, the outburst of "Amen" certainly gave them a start.

"And just in case you are wondering about those who cannot read, or parts of the world who will never see a missionary or hear the words of this Bible, I ask you to turn to Romans chapter 1 verse 20." Bud Afton gave a pause to turn the pages of his Bible as well as the congregation. "It reads: For the invisible things of him from the creation of the world are clearly seen, being understood by the things that are made, even his eternal power and Godhead; so that they are without excuse:"

Bud Afton lifted up his head from reading and asked, "Who are the 'they' you may ask? Well let's read the first sentence of the next verse." All the heads of the congregation that could see a Bible turned back to the passage they had just read. "Because that, when they knew God, they glorified *him* not as God." Bud Afton didn't want to dismiss the instruction of the entire chapter but he wanted to make a point.

"Ladies and Gentlemen, God is a skilled craftsman who desires that His work be admired and not tossed recklessly in the trash heap. Nor does He want someone or something else to get the credit for what He Himself has done. Science helps us better see what we have here on this earth and in the universe that holds the planets, sun, and stars. I will ask you this, then continue on with the rest of the passages I have here for you. When you see the sun shining warming the earth and giving life to the day, who do you see? When a bee travels from plant to bush to flower to tree in its eager business of pollination, who do you see? When you see a peculiar animal or odd coloring that changes on an insect, do you see a creative craftsman or a genetic mistake?"

Bud Afton's soft friendly voice began to crescendo to a loud proclamation with his next words. "Ladies and Gentleman, brothers and sisters in Christ; I tell you that if I believe in a man who claimed he was God's only begotten son to die on the cross for my sin and behavior of sinning, then rise from the grave three days later, that all I have to do is believe in him and gain a free ticket to heaven, leaving this sin cursed earth and sinful people, that I have access to a friend who will never leave me nor forsake me, where in the midst of any tragedy or difficulty I can have peace that passes all human understanding; then YES I can believe that God has by the mere mention of his voice and thought, created everything in space, time, and dimension and every variation of rock, tree, bug, animal and human being. I can believe we were created and not soul-less shells developed from a slug to only exist mindlessly until we die and return to the ashes of dirt!" Bud Afton slammed his fist down on the pulpit in revolt of the recent movement to deny the existence of God that would soon rain down on every corner of the nation he loved.

Shouts of "Amen" again echoed to the rafters of this little country church. The O'Brien brood looked around at each other with the conflict either fleeing the disturbing unorthodox religious scene or join in the cheers.

Bud Afton returned to his message once the cheers died down about God's forgiveness and the price Christ made on the cross for every individual who would walk this earth. Clarence, however, had fixed his eyes on the simple cross behind the pulpit. It was not like the other crosses he had seen. He had always seen a man's stretched out arms pinned at the hands or wrists and feet pinned together and knees slightly bent. The head was drooping down with a ring of a thorny band resting around the temple and the back of the head.

A voice spoke within Clarence's mind that he had never heard before.

"Why are you here, Clarence?" The voice kindly asked.

"I don't know. It sounded like a good idea." Clarence answered back without moving his lips or uttering a sound.

"Why did you bring your family here?"

"I thought it might do 'em some good." Clarence's eyes narrowed in courage to ask for a much needed answer. "Why did you take Forrey from us? You have stolen from him a life he was meant to live. He won't ever be a husband or a father or anything else for that matter. Why?!"

"Would you be here if Forrey was alive and had asked you to come?" The voice held no frustration to the grief and innocence of the question.

Clarence made no answer, he knew the answer and it was "no." Clarence knew well that he would still be perched on his seat at the City Club.

"Many a man has fought and died for the freedom of a nation and its people. Seldom will one dare to die for the freedom of the soul of an individual person." The voice needed to give no explanation as Clarence wrinkled his eyebrows at the remark but the voice continued to explain anyway.

"I take no joy in seeing men in bondage to other men. I created man so that he may walk with me in freedom. Freedom is not for you to live your life selfishly as that in itself is bondage. Nothing gives me greater pain than to see man choose a bondage that was never intended for him."

A kind, gentle, sacred hand reached out openly in Clarence's mind. "Will you trust me, Clarence? Will you believe I am who I say I am? What I did was for you just as I have done for every soul born on this earth. I am the Way. I am the Truth. I am the only door you need."

Clarence's heart began to beat rapidly. The blood in his veins seemed to scream at him for an answer. It was as if a knife soaked in honey was waiting to cut away every bad thought, every mistake, every regret, every sin from infancy to grave. Hope sat upon Clarence's shoulder waiting to refresh his pores.

"But, I'm not worth anything. You can't seriously want me?" Clarence dropped his head not wanting to believe what he asked would be true.

"I wouldn't be talking to you if I didn't want you Clarence. There is not one soul on this earth that I don't want. The question is not whether I want you, but rather do you want me?" The question of the voice disappeared at a flash of light.

Clarence was unaware that Bud Afton gave the pulpit back to the pastor of the church. The entire congregation stood up as the pastor asked if anyone would like to come forward and trust Christ to be their Savior as the piano player and organist began the introduction of the song the congregation would sing.

Clarence stepped out of the pew without fully listening to the pastor or realizing that anyone else was even still in the pews. He wouldn't know that any of his family were praying the same prayer until after he stood up from kneeling at the altar, and having said a heartfelt prayer with a man from the church who had knelt beside him. In fact, Nell and the seven oldest children as well as his new son-in-law had all come down to pray and choose Christ as their Savior.

Never before had Charlie and Clarence embraced, but today they did. Charlie renewed his commitment to Christ his Lord to be the spiritual leader of his home that Christ wanted him to be. Avelle could only cry and laugh as she embraced each of her family members and committed further to cherish the letter Forrey had not only sent her but her father as well. Sixty years later Avelle's will stated that she be buried with her Bible and Forrey's letter.

In heaven the celebration ensued. The stars would all be brighter in the night sky. The Angels sang out, "Hallelujah", with all of the strength within themselves. Forrey leapt upon the streets of gold like a schoolboy whose team had won the championship. There was no regret in him for not having the opportunity to live a full life on earth, he was living a full life right where he was. Christ beamed with pride as Gabriel wrote down the new names in the book of life, and the Holy Spirit made his dwelling place in each of their lives. Satan indeed lost some of his pawns that morning but vowed to return to remind them of their sin and taunt them with new temptations.

This was one of my Granna's favorite family stories. Every time she told me this story she would always end it with; "When the rain falls and clouds mar the sky may it be said that the friend that sticks closer than a brother is holding a big yellow umbrella over the soul's head."

Then she would kiss my forehead, say "Good night my princess", and leave my bedroom door cracked open with the white lamp that used to sit on her night stand now left on its lowest glow next to me.

The End

# ABOUT THE AUTHORS

WYNETTE I. MELLEN was born eight short months after her grandmother's death and was given her name. Her father is a retired Engineer for the Union Pacific Railroad and is now active in NARVE, an organization that is made up of retired railroad employees. Wynette is a graduate of Nampa High School and attended classes at Boise State University, though never decided on a degree. She has traveled to Peru and Albania before getting married in 2001 and is now raising three girls, which includes fraternal twins. Wynette has had several home businesses and owned a coffee shop for eight months. She now chooses to stay home to take care of her family and devote her time to them, writing and learning the art of wordsmith, and being active in her local church.

A. WYNETTE ROBERTSON was born in 1913 in Buhl, Idaho. Her father was the Section Foreman for the Union Pacific Railroad in Buhl. Her father became the Section Foreman in King Hill, Idaho in 1934. Two short years later she married Robert E. Robertson who was also working for the Union Pacific Railroad and his career path would lead him to become an Engineer. Her life on this earth was only fifty-eight years but her legacy of love and character still ripples down through to her grandchildren. Robert's grandfather came out from Colorado where his family had a sawmill and homesteaded in King Hill when Idaho was still a part of the Oregon Territory. He hired on with the Railroad when the tracks where being laid. Wynette Robertson married Robert at the age of seventeen, a year before she would graduate from high school. Although she cut her formal education short and despite the lack of professional education in the art of wordsmith, Wynette never lost her passion for the English Language. Wynette Robertson was a self-taught writer. Everyday she would read and write and write and read. She began writing letters to the Editor of the Idaho Statesman about community and political topics that interested her. Eventually she began sending poems to the Idaho Statesman to be published. While publishing her poems, she would ride the train frequently to Boise to meet with other writers which eventually became the Idaho Writers Guild. Unfortunately the lack of professional education hindered her involvement in the Guild and her success as a writer. The Novel, Railroad Redemption, has come from a novel she wrote that has been hidden away for forty years.

My grandmother dreamed. She never stopped dreaming, no matter what obstacle she faced. She dreamed of love and children. She dreamed of being a blessing to God and the people who were living around her. She helped others to dream. When her dreams began to darken, the fruit of the love she shared with others returned to her to give her strength, thereby adding new oil to light her dreams again.

My father told me that my grandmother knew my mother was pregnant with me, her second child, before she passed away. She had been sick for a while and maybe, just maybe, she thought about the others and me that would follow. Maybe she, in the end, began to pray that her dream would not die with her.

My entire life I have heard stories about my remarkable grandmother. I was told how everyone loved her, how kind she was to others and how she was someone people could lean on for support and encouragement.

I was given her name and I always knew I was given something very special; a gift, a love, even, a legacy. I envied my older cousins for being old enough to hold cherished memories of her in their heart. I pitied my younger cousins and myself for missing out on her spoiling, wisdom, and guidance.

One story I heard over and over again was the joy she had at putting her pen to paper. I heard how her short stories and poems were published in the state's newspaper and that she had attempted several novels. Her dreams of being a published author of novels would be her legacy.

Three weeks before her death, my grandmother received a crushing blow. Her novel written in inspiration of her son, my father, during his time in Vietnam would not be published. And my answer to that is:

# OH YES IT WILL

STONEHOUSE INK
www.thestonepublishinghouse.com